degrees OF GUILT

kyra's story
{DANDI DALEY MACKALL}

one plays a part . . .

miranda's story
{MELODY CARLSON}

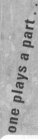

tyrone's story
{SIGMUND BROUWER}

{tyrone's story}

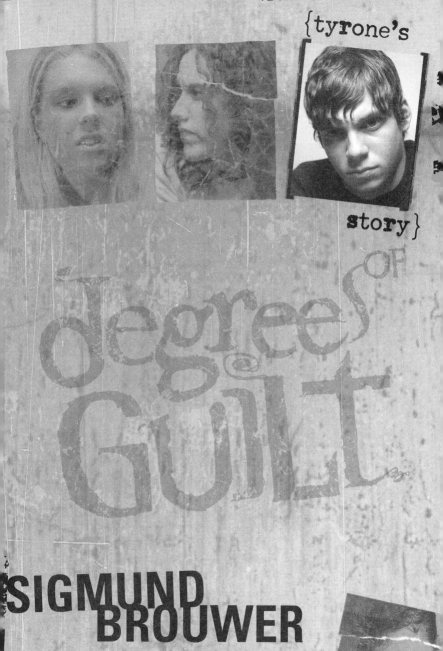

{tyrone's

story}

degrees OF

GUILT

SIGMUND BROUWER

thirsty ™

Tyndale House Publishers, Inc.
Wheaton, Illinois

Library of Congress Cataloging-in-Publication Data

Brouwer, Sigmund, date.
    Tyrone's story / Sigmund Brouwer.
        p. cm. — (The degrees of guilt series)
Summary: Eighteen-year-old Tyrone Larson ponders the events of his life that led to his part in the death of a high school friend from a drug overdose.
    ISBN 0-8423-8285-2 (pbk.)
    [1. High schools—Fiction. 2. Schools—Fiction. 3. Conduct of life—Fiction. 4. Drug traffic—Fiction. 5. Iowa—Fiction.] I. Title. II. Series.
PZ7.B79984 Tyr 2003
[Fic]—dc22   2003010943

Printed in the United States of America

07 06 05 04 03
7   6   5   4   3   2   1

(now)

"Good night, sweet prince, and flights
of angels sing thee to thy rest."

Hamlet, Act V, Scene 2

Whatever anyone tells you about Sammy
James and the night he died, it's a lie. Because I
know the truth.

Not that I'm going to tell the cops.

It's Monday morning, 10 days after Sammy died.
I'm sitting in a math class, contemplating a theory
about life that essentially says it's a highway and
too many of us become roadkill because we're too
dumb to realize what's behind the bright lights that
mesmerize us, when that chubby middle-aged secretary from the principal's office knocks on the door
and hands Mr. Gimble a note.

Gimble adjusts his bifocals and strains to read
the note, then tells us that Tyrone Larson and Hale
Ramsey are requested at the office.

Low murmurs go through the class.

That shows how little Gimble pays attention.
He's already checked off class attendance and
should know that Hale didn't make it to math this
morning. The rest of us know he's already skipped
the first two classes of the day. For that matter,
Hale didn't make it to school at all, something that
doesn't surprise me after the events of the last two
weeks.

Some of the murmurs, I'm sure, are because of
that. No one has seen Hale since Friday night.

The other murmurs, I guess, are for me.

Tyrone Larson. Eighteen. About to graduate from
Macon High. Three claims to fame. Quiet science
brain. Quiet son of a religious man now in jail. Quiet
field-goal kicker for the Macon Tigers. Mostly I'm
the invisible guy at Macon High. The way I like it
and the way I work to keep it. I'm so weird on the
inside that I think it's smarter to keep my mouth
shut and have people *wonder* if I'm weird than to
open my mouth and prove it.

Gimble calls my name again.

I stand.

Miranda Sanchez—tall, athletic, and good-looking
with serious blue eyes—glances at me, then snaps
her eyes back to her books real fast.

Sammy had it for her bad.

I think she had it bad for him too.

But they never got the chance to see where it
would take them.

Kyra James, Sammy's twin sister, keeps her head
down and doesn't look my way. She's blonde and
does that whole cheerleader thing, except she's got

a brain. And even though she's dated nearly every eligible male at Macon High, including me, doesn't have a reputation for being easy.

Kyra was best friends with Miranda, but Sammy dying the way he did has messed them up. They don't talk anymore.

Kyra won't talk to me either. Same reason. Sammy dying the way he did.

I tell myself I don't care about her silence. That it doesn't matter. After all, last New Year's Eve I had my big chance with her and blew it. Because I let her have a glimpse of the weirdness inside me.

But as much as I tell myself otherwise, I do care. So it's just as well she keeps her face hidden as I stand. For every time I see her eyes and her smile, it makes me want to find a white horse and a lance and go conquer a fire-breathing dragon. It's some-thing she doesn't know, something the world doesn't know, and something I intend to keep hidden.

I walk to the front, to the door.

As I get halfway up my row, Brianna Devereaux, the class flirt, blows me a kiss and whispers, "Hurry back, baby!" in this low sexy Marilyn Monroe voice loud enough to make a couple guys nearby laugh. Partly because of how she said it, partly because it's funny that someone like her would publicly show that kind of interest in someone like me.

I'm the science whiz. She's the blonde bombshell.

Like Kyra, she's a cheerleader, but unlike Kyra, Brianna makes every bad cliché about cheerleaders true. Her well-deserved reputation for what happens when she's alone with a guy is a little different than

Kyra's. No, a lot different. No wonder Kyra and Brianna don't get along.

There's plenty about Brianna and me I don't want the world to know, either. But with what's happened in the last two weeks, I doubt I'll win the fight to keep all of that as easily hidden as how I still feel about Kyra.

I follow the secretary and the *swish-swish* of her panty hose down the hallway. I wrinkle my nose at the smell of cheap perfume that drifts behind her.

I'm not worried this visit to the office is something like the day that Amy Sing went down and was told her old man had just suffered a heart attack, because frankly, my old man doesn't exist for me. I figure if he did have a heart attack, it would make him the first roadkill that makes sense in my life.

Instead, I'm worried—for good reason—that it's about Sammy.

And my involvement in his death.

Sammy is gone.

On the highway of life he stepped into the embrace of bright headlights at a party—his first— less than two weeks ago. By the time anyone realized what was roaring in his direction, it was too late.

For all of us.

Nobody really understood how much a part of Macon High Sammy was until everything in our world was changed as a result of his death. Like he was the center of gravity, and now the bus is wobbling as the rest of us keep going on a one-way trip that takes us farther every day from who he was. And what he meant to us.

My role in his departure is ripping me apart with

7

guilt. And as I walk down the hallway, I'm afraid it's a guilt the rest of the world will soon discover.

■   ■   ■

Sure enough, in the office there's a cop waiting for me, some guy with a big belly.

I recognize him because he sets up speed traps just down the road and lets the businessmen who can afford the tickets whiz by while he waits to nab all the teenage drivers who are desperately escaping our high school prison after the final buzzer of the day.

Now the cop speaks to me in a low, sympathetic voice that he probably thinks is going to fool me. "We need you for some routine questions," he says, and eyes me.

I'm in a bad mood. Of course, I've been in that kind of a mood since the night Sammy died. No, if I'm going to be honest with myself, I've been in a bad mood since long before that, with nobody to blame but myself.

Now, to make it worse, I know this cop's lying to me. Who actually gets pulled out of class for routine questions? Am I stupid? Well, that's the way he's treating me. And I'm about done with acting like I'm Teflon, so that stuff just rolls off my back. Ever since Sammy died, things seem to be sticking.

"Routine questions?" I say. "I guess that means you're looking for routine answers. How much use could that be for anyone?"

He stares at me.

The secretary, who was pretending to be busy with some memos, looks up at me. Her mouth is open. We live in a small town, where everybody knows everybody. And that means everybody knows I'm a cynic. But in this situation, I can tell the secretary thinks I'm taking the smart-mouth attitude just a little too far. She's probably right. Still, I smile at the cop, amazed at how good it feels to really vent. I don't usually say much around school.

Now I notice that the cop's hands are twitching, like he wants to wrap them around my neck. I have this image of him screaming as he rushes forward to rip me apart. And for some reason, I want to egg him on. To see what he'll really do if he's pushed.

So I say, "Is that doughnut dust around your lips?"

"What's that, kid?" His face turns mean.

"Doughnut dust," I deadpan. "The white sugary stuff. It's a dead giveaway that you just got here from a coffee shop."

His hands keep twitching.

"I had it in my mind we were going to speak privately someplace here in the school," he says. "But now I think I'll take you down to the station."

"Let me call a lawyer," I say. I should be afraid. I've been through more than my share of cops and lawyers because of my dad going to prison. And I know more about Sammy's death than I want to. But I've turned my fear into a wave of anger. It feels good to surf this wave. I pull my cell phone out of my pocket.

"Need one?" he asks, still trying to out-tough me.

But I realize something.

Now that the worst has happened, just the way I expected and dreaded, I've got nothing to lose. A person with nothing to lose doesn't care. And someone who doesn't care is a bad person to fight. Suddenly that's me.

"I'm a TV kid," I tell him. "That's where we get our role models. Watch any cop show. Everyone demands a lawyer."

I start punching numbers, like I know exactly who to call.

The cop doesn't say a word. Just pushes me out the door.

My phone still to my ear, I pick up the latest sports news on this service I subscribe to.

The cop escorts me to his police car in the parking lot. All the kids in my math class are now staring out the window and watching me get in the backseat. I can already hear the gossip when they talk about it later. Because they will. That's the way life in Macon, Iowa, works.

Then I go.

I, Tyrone Larson, am being taken away in a
police cruiser because of decisions I've made since
the beginning of the year. I'm not going to duck that,
not going to blame anybody else. I have nobody to
blame but myself.

I brought this upon myself, decided on the paths
that led me here. I never thought I'd be cruising
town in the back of a police car.

But I can legitimately argue that those paths
would not have been in front of me—or Hale Ramsey
or Kyra James or Miranda Sanchez or even Brianna
Devereaux—without one person, whose arrival at
Macon High on the Monday morning after New
Year's Day hit all of us with the impact and flash
of a meteor.

Mr. Mitchell Wade.

He's the catalyst.

It shows something, I guess, that I would think of him that way. But I can't help it.

You may think high school chemistry is boring. In fact, you probably *should* think it's boring, because in an MTV world there's not much that's cool about a white-coated teacher with pocket protectors for his pens who stands in front of a bunch of hormone-crazed kids and tries to explain Avogadro's number or electron pair theory.

Unfortunately for me, that's part of my weird-ness. I happen to like chemistry and physics and just about anything else that involves science.

We live in an unpredictable world. Something I don't like.

We live in a world that doesn't seem to make sense. Something else I don't like.

Science? Once you figure it out, you can predict things. And the explanations make sense. In science, then, the world makes sense. I like that.

To me, there's something very comforting about the black-and-white precision and utter pre-dictability of chemical reactions. It's like two plus two always equaling four anywhere in the universe, at any point in time. It's a truth that is rock solid and unchangeable. Chemistry and physics are just like that, except on a grander and far more compli-cated scale. Chemical reactions are a beautiful dance of electrons and protons and subatomic particles—all bound by four basic laws: gravity, electromagnetism, and strong and weak nuclear forces. It's a dance so intricate it's almost beyond comprehension. And always, always unchangeable.

I know, weird to get this excited about stuff like that.

Kyra James thought the same thing on New Year's Eve, the night that I blew my big chance with her. When we looked up and saw the stars, I started to explain the difference between nuclear fission and nuclear fusion, and how I thought it was cool that stars were so big that the resulting gravity put so much force on the hydrogen atoms they actually fused and the by-product was energy.

"See," I'd said, all serious and enthusiastic, "all of the energy in this universe is created by gravity, the weakest force known to physics, and nobody can explain why or how gravity works the way it does. Cool, huh?"

And she'd said in a dry voice, "Wow, and here I thought the stars were all about poetry and romance."

So if I can turn a romantic moment into a science lecture, it shouldn't surprise anyone that I think of Mitchell Wade as a catalyst.

In chemistry a catalyst is a substance that increases the speed of a reaction without being consumed by the reaction. Like the conversion of ozone into oxygen, normally a very slow process. But if there happens to be some nitric oxide around, look out. The nitric-oxide molecule combines with an oxygen atom to make nitrogen dioxide. Then nitrogen dioxide reacts with ozone and makes two molecules of oxygen. What's cool—at least to me— is that the second step of the reaction leaves exactly as much nitric oxide as was burned by the first step, and the process begins again. The catalyst is still there, but what's around it has changed.

That's Mitchell Wade.

Catalyst.

Someone whose presence increased the interactions of the people around him, but who was basically untouched by all of the reactions that occurred because of him. The same before and, it seems, the same after.

While the rest of us changed with no hope of return.

Which, looking back, made one of his first statements to us all the more remarkable.

A partial lie, a partial prophecy, but most definitely remarkable.

■ ■ ■

I'm thinking those thoughts about Mitchell Wade as we arrive at the police station and I'm escorted into a small bare room that smells like sweat and stale coffee. The big-bellied cop grunts and points toward a small bare table that's bolted to the floor. Like anybody would even think of stealing it.

I brush crumbs off the seat and sit down, wondering how long of a wait I'll have before the interrogation begins. My watch beeps as I click a button on its side.

Finally, a woman walks into the room. "Tyrone, I'm Detective Sanders," she says, reaching over to shake my hand. "I understand you've called for a lawyer?"

She doesn't look much different than what I imagine my own mother would have looked like if she were still alive. Middle-aged. Short sandy hair. Brown eyes. A tired face.

I shrug in response to her question. I peer down at the stopwatch function on my watch.

"Nine minutes, 32 seconds," I tell her. "That's how long I've been sitting at this table."

"I was busy," she says.

"That's a lot of femtoseconds to make me wait," I say.

"Femtoseconds." Not a question. She merely repeats what I said, as if understanding that I will explain.

Femtoseconds are something I had just read about the night before in one of the science magazines I subscribe to. So I explain. "There are as many femtoseconds in a single second as there are seconds in 32 million years.

"I find that interesting because molecular bonds form and break on timescales measured in femtoseconds. And since the thought process of your brain relies on the breaking and forming of those molecular bonds as chemicals diffuse from one nerve synapse to another, I also wonder how much slower we would think if the process took 10 times longer. Or a hundred times longer.

"Just think about thinking. . . . If you think slower, your nerve impulses are slower. You'd walk slower, have slower reactions.

"Or, on the other hand, are we walking and talking in slow motion compared to what it would be like if molecular bonds formed and broke 10 times faster?

"And what laws predetermine the speed of chemical reactions on a molecular level? Can those laws be changed? And if they can't be changed, does that mean each of us is a prisoner of our chemical makeup? That we're predestined to certain actions in life? That we can't help who we are, or change anything we do?"

Surprised at how much I've said aloud, I stop to take a breath. Then I remember pieces of sermons I've heard over the years, at least back when my father and I used to go to church. All about how important it is to make good decisions, to choose the "right path" in life.

Yeah, right. Like my father really listened, I thought.

I continue my musing aloud to the detective. "Or can we make decisions that will change our life path? Decisions that will affect what we do now and in the future? And wouldn't that mean—?"

"Thank you very much, Ty," Detective Sanders says, interrupting my flow of words and questions. "I feel I'm more knowledgeable now than I was before you began."

I cock my head, trying to figure out if she's being sarcastic.

"I'd also like to expand my knowledge in terms of your request for a lawyer," she continues. "The officer who escorted you here mentioned something about it."

"I didn't call for a lawyer," I say to Detective

Sanders. I scrutinize my watch again. I reset it and
start the stopwatch function again. Hoping she'll get
the hint.

I refrain from mentioning how many more quadrillions of femtoseconds have passed since she entered
the room. Or how many chemical reactions have
occurred in her brain and mine during the thoughts
it has taken to say all we have until this point.

I also dread what might be spoken during the
next quadrillions and quadrillions of femtoseconds.
Maybe that's why we measure time at a slower pace.
Quadrillions of femtoseconds seems like forever
compared to just a couple of minutes.

"Of course you didn't call for a lawyer," she
says as she sits opposite me and sets down a tape
recorder and a notepad. "We took your cell phone.
There's no phone in here."

She gives me a tight smile like she just made
a joke.

I oblige by giving her a tight smile in return.

"I'm asking for the record," she says, now that
each of us has established our reputation as a come-
dian for the other. "Would you like a lawyer?
Really, I have your best interests in mind here."

Her tone is even. I can almost believe she truly
is nice. Not like big-belly, who did a bad job of
faking it.

The obvious response is to ask her if I need a
lawyer. That's how it would happen on television.
Instead, I say, "No thanks."

"Are you sure? We can get you one, state
appointed."

Bottom of the barrel, of course.

"I'm sure," I say. "Ninety-nine percent of them give the other one percent a bad name."

She catches the implication immediately and smiles.

Normally I would have kept that thought to myself. The lawyer joke. But I'm feeling reckless.

"I just want to talk to you about the party that took place at the residence of Miranda Sanchez," Detective Sanders says. "Do you mind if I tape this conversation?"

I shrug again.

"I'll take that as a yes," she says. "Unless you say otherwise."

I don't say otherwise.

She starts the tape recorder. She states the date and time and my name and that I'll be talking with full knowledge the conversation is being taped. She plays back a few seconds to make sure the recorder is working. When she's satisfied, she sets it back down on the table. The unblinking red light of the recorder stares at me.

"First of all," she says. "Are you thirsty? Can I get you a glass of water? You don't look like a smoker. Otherwise I'd offer you a cigarette."

"Diplomacy," I say, "is the art of saying 'good doggie' while looking for a bigger stick."

"I beg your pardon, Tyrone?"

"I can picture you being nice to me until that doesn't work."

She sighs. "This is Macon, Iowa. Not some TV cop show. All I've got are a few questions for you.

A great kid named Samuel James died under unusual circumstances. It's my job to find out why."

Inside, I wince. I didn't need the reminder of why I was here. For the past 10 days I've thought of nothing else. But outside I stay cool. I nod. "A good scapegoat is often better than a solution to a problem."

Nice as she is, I enjoy seeing anger flash across her face. Maybe that should tell me that life is more fun if you take chances instead of just sitting on the sidelines, watching things happen around you. Or maybe it's just because I'm miserable and afraid and angry about being miserable and afraid.

She composes herself and speaks calmly. "If I can find out why it happened, maybe that will prevent it from happening again. I really, really wish it could be different. That it had never happened and that you were still back in math class and that I was stuck in a patrol car with a partner whose bad breath makes me want to wear a gas mask."

She wants me to smile with that statement, and I can't help myself. I think of a cop driving around town with a gas mask and I smile.

It also gets me thinking about an article I read once on how many different kinds of colonies of bacteria live in our bodies, including the bacteria on our tongues and teeth that cause bad breath. Millions and millions of living creatures. On our teeth, tongues, inside our intestines, under our armpits. We're an entire ecosystem for the little parasites. Wouldn't do any good to get rid of them;

we need them as badly as they need us. But it's just not pleasant, thinking about being a host for all those colonies.

"How about it," she says. "Drop the wise-guy act and just talk to me."

I don't agree. But I don't disagree.

"You and Mitchell Wade were at the party the night that Samuel James died, right?"

I'm glad she didn't say *expired*. *Dead* is a brutal word. But true. Dead is so final a person shouldn't pretend it's anything else by using different words to try to soften it.

I nod. Mitchell Wade and I were both at the party.

"Would you mind," she says softly, "answering out loud? The tape recorder doesn't pick up body language."

"I was there. At the party." Why deny it? Detective Sanders would know that from talking to other people who were there. "So was Mitchell Wade."

The big question is this: What does she know about Mitchell Wade and me and our involvement in Sammy's death?

The scary thing is, this isn't the only death I've been involved in. . . .

I killed my mother.

Really.

She died while she was giving birth to me. I'm told there came a point during labor where the doctors told her that it would come down to a simple decision. If they eliminated the risk to her health, there was a good chance I'd be deprived of oxygen so long that I might be born with brain damage, or would even die. But if they ensured my health, there was an equal risk she would be harmed.

I'm also told that she was adamant that the baby inside her—me—would not face any risks, no matter how much risk it meant for her.

She died an hour after I was born. She never even had a chance to hold me.

Much as I'm interested in science and how things

work, that's one thing I've never tried to find out. The exact details of what went wrong as she sacrificed her life to bring me into the world.

I'm fine with that now.

Really.

There was a time I wasn't.

I was 13 when my father was sent to prison. For a couple of years after, I was a very unadjusted kid. In fact, that's why my stepmother sent me to Macon to live with her mother, which makes her my stepgrandmother.

Before I was sent away, during the rough months with my stepmother in Chicago after my father was gone, I was forced to spend time with a psychiatrist three times a week, one hour per session. The psychiatrist spent most of his time getting me to talk about my sense of guilt about killing my mother. He told me I had unresolved issues about her death.

I told him that anyone would feel lousy about having someone sacrifice his or her life so that you can live. But that didn't mean I had issues.

I fought that for appointment after appointment until I finally realized he wasn't going to let it go. The smart thing to do at that point was resolve those issues. So I let him discuss it with me until he was convinced I didn't feel anything lousy about killing my mother.

Which I guess now means I'm fine with it. And for anyone who doesn't believe me, there's a whole file of reports in a psychiatrist's office in Chicago that says otherwise.

Here's the deal.

Sitting with Detective Sanders gets me thinking about my mother, simply because Detective Sanders has that worn, comfortable look about her that I imagine good mothers have when dealing with the weariness of life and all the problems of their children.

But now, suddenly, after her question about Mitchell Wade, Detective Sanders makes a subtle shift, and she doesn't look as worn and comfortable anymore.

She's begun to look more like a predator.

■   ■   ■

As the femtoseconds flash by in the quadrillions, Detective Sanders lets the tension stretch. Her awareness, it seems, is heightened in that predator way.

I decide she's waiting me out, hoping it will scare me into blurting something I shouldn't.

Like about Hale, my best friend—correction, my *former* best friend. He's a hillbilly. Literally. Knows about nature and stuff because of how and where he was raised. He told me that when hawks soar high above the ground, they'll scream once in a while and try to scare hidden rabbits into bolting into plain sight.

Sitting behind that bare table in the police station, I make my own shift.

Not as subtle.

I stop thinking of Detective Sanders as someone

that my mother might have looked like. Instead
I think of her as a hawk, waiting to swoop down
on me. In my mind I cower under a protective bush.
I don't say a word.

It feels like a minor victory when Detective
Sanders gives up trying to make me bolt and picks
up her notepad and flips through it.

"Were you wearing a black T-shirt at the party?"

"I'm not a girl," I say. "I can't tell you what I
wore yesterday, let alone a couple of weeks ago.
Nor can I tell you where I bought it and how much
it cost there and at the three other places I shopped
and didn't buy it."

No smile from her at my clumsy attempt at
humor.

"Black T-shirt," she says, still reading from the
notebook. "You were wearing it inside out."

Again that's something she could confirm. I have
this stand about corporate logos. If corporations
want me to advertise for them, they should pay me.
Like Nike. They expect me to buy the shirt or the
jacket that carries their logo. Not right. I won't do
it. The black T-shirt with a Nike logo on it was a
Christmas gift. Since I didn't get a check from
Nike to become a walking billboard on their behalf,
I wasn't going to let the world see their logo. That's
what's a pain about my stand. It takes hours to
remove the embroidery of a logo. When I'm in a
hurry, I just wear the shirt inside out. Like on the
night of the party where Sammy died.

"That would have been me," I say. "Didn't have
time to remove the threads."

She doesn't ask what I mean by that. Which tells me she already knows about my weird stand against corporations. Which tells me that someone has been talking to her about me. And that she probably already knows the answers to all her questions.

Nice as she looks, I suddenly know for sure this isn't an information-gathering session. It's a trap. Designed for me.

"You spoke to Sammy that night?" she asks.

"I did," I say. Tempted as I am to answer just yes or no, I know that if I do, Detective Sanders is going to realize that I realize I'm in the middle of a trap. So I add more to my answer, talking like I want to help her out. I really should just give up and tell her all of the truth about it, but a part of me is desperate enough to believe that maybe I can find some way out over the next few weeks.

"Sammy and I were friends," I continue, feeling bad inside all over again at even the word *friends*. Sammy and I had just started to hang out more together. But now he was dead, and I'd never have that chance again. Every time I thought about it, I felt a tiny pinch inside. As if someone had snipped a tiny piece out of one of my veins. "It would have been strange if I didn't talk to him," I finish.

"Friends don't offer friends drugs," she says, watching me carefully.

"No," I say, "they don't."

I glance at my stopwatch. It's only been seven minutes and 10 seconds. Seems like a lot more. Especially in femtoseconds.

"Let me ask you directly," she says, boring her

eyes into mine. "Did you give Sammy any pills at the party?"

This is crunch time. All along I knew this question was coming. If I evade the question, after answering all the others, it's as good as telling her I did it but don't want to admit it. Plus I have this thing about lying. I hate it.

I give her the truth, guessing it might surprise her. "Yes."

She's good. Doesn't even blink. "What kind of pills?"

"Aspirin. He said he had a headache."

"You carry aspirin with you everywhere?"

"No. I stole them. From the bathroom at the party."

This doesn't even slow her down. "Did you give him any other pills?"

"No. Just the aspirin."

She pauses, then says softly, "Tyrone, holding back now is only going to make it worse for you when the truth comes out. Give me truth."

"Two wrongs don't make a right," I say. "But three lefts do."

"Pardon me?"

"The lottery is a tax on people who are bad at math."

"You're not making sense."

"You wanted truth and I gave you two truths. Turning left three times is like making a right. Lottery money profits go to the state, which makes it like a tax, and the only people who contribute are the ones who are so bad at math they don't or can't calculate the miniscule odds of winning. I don't see how anyone can disagree with either statement. Ergo . . . truth."

I like that word. *Ergo.* Latin for "therefore." As in *cogito ergo sum.* Which translates to "I think, therefore I am."

Strange how a person's mind will wander when it shouldn't. I feel giddy with the danger in front of me. Maybe it's like the feeling you have on skis, moving at full speed when you know you can't stop. What a rush . . . until you go over the cliff.

"Tyrone . . ." She pauses as if she's going to say one thing, then changes her mind. "Where's Hale Ramsey?"

This one is easy to answer truthfully. "I don't know."

"When was the last time you saw him?"

"Friday. Three days ago."

"Did he tell you his plans for the weekend?"

I shake my head. Remember how my friend had betrayed me. "No," I say.

"But he's your friend. Surely if he was going somewhere, he'd tell you."

"That's where you're wrong. He's not my friend."

She consults her notebook again.

I sense the interview is nearly over. I check my stopwatch.

Ten minutes and 12 seconds. Millions upon millions of chemical reactions have occurred in my brain as nerve synapses fired at a speed that can only be accurately measured in femtoseconds.

"Tell me," she says casually. "What happened to your car?"

I flinch. This isn't a question I expected.

"I understand," she says, lifting her head and eyeing me directly, "that it appears to have been beaten by hail. Bumps everywhere."

By now I've recovered from my obvious flinch in front of her.

At least I hope and think I've recovered. I'm studying her, trying to guess if what she means is *hail,* as in the big white ice chunks falling from the sky. If she doesn't know the truth about what happened to my car, her choice of words would be hilarious. Except there is nothing funny about any of this.

"My car has always been ugly," I say.

"Ugly? Or vandalized? We haven't had a hail-storm recently. You can report these things to the police."

"Ugly," I repeat. Glad to find out she did mean *hail.*

"I understand as well," she says, lifting her head and peering directly at me again, "that you and Hale spend a lot of time together."

"*Spent* time with him," I said. "Not spend. Spent. Past tense. We aren't friends anymore."

There is a lot of truth in that.

Too much truth.

He's as tied into all of this as Mitchell Wade is. Maybe more.

Along with Kyra and Miranda and Brianna and Sammy himself.

It's a long story, and although most of what happened began in January, barely a few months ago,
in another way, years earlier, all of our lives inter-
sected to begin the journey to the final road that led
to Sammy's death.

If only I'd known then what I know now.

Really.

(then)

"Men at some time are masters of their fates."

Julius Caesar, Act I, Scene 2

Macon, Iowa, is a small town. The kind of town where farmers actually drive tractors to the post office and the women trade recipes down at the local grocery store. I did not grow up here, of course. I grew up in Chicago, in an area of luxury high-rises that overlooked Lake Michigan.

It wasn't until my freshman year that I arrived in Macon, straight from a private school in Chicago where we all wore identical school uniforms and demerits were issued for shirts, ties, or pants that weren't sufficiently ironed free of any wrinkles. No wonder, huh, that I've decided to wear what I like when I like, even if that means turning shirts inside out to hide the corporate labels.

Any new school is tough to crack. It's tough enough to go from an elite private school to a rowdy public school. But imagine what it's like on the first day when basically all the other students have known each other their entire lives.

Because that was Macon High. Small, filled with classes where all the students had been in the same classes together since their kindergarten years.

It took me six months to find my niche, to stake it out, and to protect it so that at least I was accepted as part of the scenery. Not that I fit in. But I was accepted for not fitting in.

I wasn't alone in feeling like a stranger on that first day. There was one other person new to the school.

Hale Ramsey.

Who would immediately share my misery.

And, I was to find out later, much much more.

■   ■   ■

Hale Ramsey.

A little over four years earlier, on my first day in school as a freshman, I'd walked into English class to find him hanging on the wall from a coat hook.

Back then he was one of the smallest guys in the high school. In fact, back then, there was only one guy smaller. Me.

Seeing the strange sight, I should have turned around immediately and fled the classroom.

But I was stunned by the sight of Hale motionless on the coat hook, black silent rage across his narrow face. He had a mullet cut—short hair in front, long hair at the back. His skin was pocked. He wore a Harley-Davidson T-shirt and had a tattoo of a black widow on his skinny right bicep. I did not know it, but he too had moved to Macon that summer. This was also *his* first day among the kids of a small town who had all grown up together.

He must have sensed by my bewilderment that I was new to the school too.

"Git," he said to me, the twang of his hillbilly upbringing obvious in that one word. I didn't realize he was trying to give me warning.

I turned my head slightly and saw a group of guys in the back of the room, grinning.

Jocks, I knew immediately. Jocks always hang in packs.

"Git," Hale repeated. "Ah'm telling ya—"

As I tried to sort through the situation, a powerful arm wrapped around me from behind.

I smelled Old Spice aftershave.

I heard a mixture of a giggle and a grunt as I was tilted sideways, off balance.

Immediately I felt the owner of that powerful arm pull the shirt out of the back of my pants with his other hand.

I kicked and squirmed, but it was useless. He yanked the top of my underwear out of the back of my pants.

Then I was airborne, facing the ground. One hand held my collar, the other hand held the top of my underwear.

Then I was lifted in one smooth motion, spun around before I could swing out at my attacker, pushed up against the wall, and dropped a few inches. My underwear snagged a coat hook beside Hale Ramsey.

From up on the wall, like a piece of artwork, I was given the opportunity for my first look at my attacker.

D.J. Johnson. Wearing a faded jean jacket that matched in color his tight jeans. He had dark hair and a wide, handsome face, now twisted with suppressed mirth. He was large and strong and supple. I'd find out later he played fullback. As a freshman, he was a starter on the high school team. He was amazingly athletic, as evidenced by the smoothness with which he'd impaled me on the coat hook by my underwear. And amazingly stupid.

Grinning, he raised his arms and flexed his biceps like a strongman in the circus. His friends in the back of the room applauded.

By now my underwear had become extremely uncomfortable.

"Don't fight," Hale whispered to me. "Don't struggle. Don't cuss. Don't give them any satisfaction at all."

I took his advice. Crossed my arms. And waited for the arrival of a teacher.

Girls began to walk into the classroom.

Among them was a blonde goddess whose face crinkled in immediate concern. Kyra James. In a skirt and a blouse and a vest. Long silky hair. Unlike me, she was not befuddled by the sight of the two of us hanging on the wall.

She looked directly at D.J. Johnson. "I know

you're behind this, D.J. Get them down. New kids or not, they don't deserve this."

"No." Hale spoke loudly enough to cut through all the giggles and murmurs and whispers. "I'll hang here for a year before I ask anyone for help."

With his arms crossed too, Hale kept a strange sort of dignity and composure. I tried to follow his example. But it was difficult, given the discomfort of my position.

Kyra, I think, understood. Humiliating as it was to be hanging on a coat hook by the back of my underwear, it would be even more humiliating to be rescued by a girl.

She took her seat without saying another word. Uncomfortable as I was, I couldn't take my eyes off her.

The jocks continued to laugh at us. Except for one tall guy who stood alone, arms folded, at the back of the room. He wasn't laughing, but he wasn't coming to our rescue either. Later I found out he was Kyra James' twin brother, Sammy.

I never would have guessed then what a role I'd play in Sammy's life, or he in mine.

"Shoot." Hale spoke to me from the side of his mouth. "I *told* my uncle I should have taken a knife to school. Then I could cut them up like bait fish."

At the beginning of our freshman year at Macon High, the differences between Hale Ramsey and me were vast.

He was hillbilly and, as I was to discover, a recent release from a juvenile detention center in London, Kentucky. I was from downtown Chicago and a home of five-course meals with folded white cloth napkins. At least that was before my father decided to embezzle funds. Now, with my father in prison and all our assets taken to repay the organization, my stepmother was struggling just to pay rent on an apartment.

Hale liked to talk. A lot.

I didn't.

He was a hot-rod guy, armed with wrenches and screwdrivers, determined to coax as much horsepower as possible from an old Camaro.

I was Mr. Science and actually owned a home chemistry set, which I admitted to no one.

In Macon he lived on a pig farm just outside of town with his aunt, uncle, and five other kids younger than he was.

In Macon I lived in a three-bedroom apartment with Gran, my stepmother's mother.

Hale dressed like a gang biker.

I used to be prep school but now was rebelling against it and my whole old lifestyle. Even more of a reason to hate labels on my clothes.

He spoke hillbilly twang with often unfathomable expressions.

I'd been taught to use English as it had been designed.

And on and on.

But the three things we had in common were enough to unite us. We were small and had yet to hit our growth spurts that would take us to slightly taller than average by twelfth grade. We were transplants to Macon, Iowa. And D.J. Johnson had become our common enemy.

Combined, Hale and I probably weighed as much as D.J. by himself, which, in theory, should have made our battles more fair. But D.J. never approached us alone, preferring to keep the odds vastly in his favor.

He traveled everywhere in the high school with his jock pack. Almost in a V-formation, with D.J. at the front and two or three others trailing behind on each side like geese in flight.

Still, that wasn't going to stop me. Or Hale.

degrees of guilt

We took our first opportunity at revenge in chemistry class later that day, the class immediately after the lunch break.

■ ■ ■

I'd gone in during the noon break to prepare what I needed. It wasn't difficult to break into the supplies cabinet of the chem lab. All I'd had to do was unscrew some hinges.

At the workstation that Hale and I would take, I set two beakers of clear liquid. One was marked *NaOH,* sodium hydroxide. The other was *HCl,* hydrochloric acid. I hid the beakers from the teacher's view with a stack of books. Beside the beakers were what looked like small chunks of rock, a small dropper, and two apples.

Then I sat at the workstation and waited for the buzzer to begin the next class period.

Hale Ramsey sauntered in with the rest of the students and made a beeline for where I sat. Not that others were crowding to join me. No, Hale and I had already been marked as losers.

D.J. and his friends smirked at us.

I kept my face bland.

Halfway through the class, Hale excused himself to go to the washroom.

A half minute later the phone rang in the classroom.

Mr. Nesbitt, an older man with wire-rim glasses and chewed fingernails, stopped his discussion on the early history of the periodic table. He answered,

42

listened a few seconds, nodded, and hung up. Then
he excused himself from the classroom.

Hale had kept up his end of the arrangement,
calling from a pay phone in the high school lobby.
It was a message for Mr. Nesbitt to go to the library
to talk to Miss Tristen about some books. And Miss
Tristen, if Hale had done it according to plan, had
just received a message to go to the office. I hoped
the confusion would give us at least five minutes
unsupervised.

Thirty seconds after Mr. Nesbitt's departure,
when conversation among all the students was just
starting to buzz through the lab, Hale reentered the
classroom.

He rejoined me.

I pulled out the two beakers.

"What y'all got?" Hale asked loudly.

"Hydrochloric acid," I said. "Watch this."

We'd spoken at a high enough volume that it
grabbed the attention of most of the students near
us. Their conversations dropped, and that in turn
drew more attention.

"Watch this," I said. I dipped the dropper into
the solution and drew it full. I squeezed the contents of the dropper on one of the apples. Immediately it blackened and dissolved, with a small curl
of vapor rising from it.

"Shoot!" Hale said. He touched the apple. Yelped.

"Hydrochloric acid," I repeated. "That'll burn
right through you. Be careful."

Hale kept yelping and shaking his finger.

Now the room was silent, all attention on us.

degrees of guilt

I dipped the dropper into the other beaker.

"Sodium hydroxide," I announced. "Just as dangerous as hydrochloric acid."

I proved it by squeezing some of the solution on the other apple. Again, the flesh of the apple sputtered and dissolved in a very satisfactory way.

"Shoot!" Hale said. He didn't reach out and touch it.

Calmly I poured the contents of one beaker into the other. Then back and forth. I left half in one beaker and half in the other.

I held one beaker at arm's length and slowly walked toward D.J. Johnson.

"You shouldn't have messed with me this morning," I said. "You don't know a thing about me."

He stood from his chair, leaving his jean jacket draped on it, and slowly backed away.

"Come on," he said. "This isn't funny."

"I'm psycho," I said. "One step short of insane. It's why I got kicked out of my last three schools."

I advanced, and he retreated more. Until his back hit the wall.

"Psycho," I repeated. "Totally psycho."

I threw the contents of the beaker into his face.

He shrieked.

He rubbed his face with his hands.

And shrieked louder as the liquid trickled into his eyes.

With one arm across his face and the other arm in front of him as if he were pushing aside tacklers, he stumbled forward.

"Help me," he shouted, "help me!"

No one moved. All of them were frozen by the horror of what they'd witnessed.

"Come on!" he shouted. "Sammy! Dylan! Someone."

I moved back to my workstation. I grabbed the other beaker. The one that contained the other half of the mixture.

His friends must have taken that as a threat, because none moved.

"I'm blind," D.J. shrieked. "Someone take me for help!"

It was Kyra who moved, who broke the frozen tableau of spectators. Perhaps she decided that even a psycho wouldn't throw acid on her. She took D.J.'s arm and guided him to the front of the room and out the door.

He clutched her, crying. "My eyes," he moaned. "They hurt. I can't see."

In the silence in the lab that followed their departure, we all clearly heard him blubbering down the hallway.

Hale snickered.

As for me, I knew that everyone else was staring at the beaker in my hand. The other half of the mixture that had blinded D.J.

I grinned.

Like a psycho.

And tilted my head back and drained all of the solution in three large gulps.

7

Sometimes I've wondered if all my weirdness came from my father. Did he spend his growing-up years stuck behind a chemistry magazine? And is that why he had such a hard time relating to others? It's hard to know, though, because I really didn't know him all that well. Sure, he was there— at least most dinners and most nights. But he was more on the fringes of my life than a part of it. Forget any father-son ball games or anything like that. It was like I was his son and he tolerated me, but didn't want to hang around me because I'd killed my mother. At least that's how I felt the last two years before he went to prison.

My father, until the day that he listened to his attorney's advice and gave himself up to the authorities who were closing in during an investigative audit, had been chief financial officer for a Christian organization dedicated to getting kids in developing countries matched with foster parents in the United States. Sick, huh? To have a father who stole funds from little kids who really needed it to pad his own wallet?

If I named that organization, I'm sure you'd be familiar with it. But it's not worth the legal trouble to actually spell out the name of it.

Not much about the details of my father's fraudulent activities made it public—part of the legal plea bargaining my father did once he knew all of his activities were about to be unraveled. In short, for reduced jail time and no lawsuit against him, he returned what money was left from what he'd diverted for himself.

The charity organization had no choice about the jail terms because my father had broken federal laws. But the organization did have a choice about declining a further lawsuit and was happy to let this trouble sink away quietly.

From the viewpoint of the organization, it was the lesser of two evils. After all, how many people would continue to send money to help foster kids if they found out instead that too much of their contributions had gone into offshore bank accounts designed to help a certain financial officer's future retirement?

The plea bargain and lawsuit deal included a strict public silence on the matter by my father and his family. Much as I'd like to deny it, family does include me, so I can't mention the name of the organization. I mean, since he's my father, I have no choice but to be his son. That's the way genetics works.

But that doesn't mean I like it. In case it isn't obvious, I don't like my father—or the fact that I'm stuck being his son. How could you like a person who prays publicly at every chance and steals privately at the same time? And not only once, but over and over and over?

Because of genetics, however, I inherited from him the same average build and average looks.

It now seems—given my part in Sammy's death—that I also inherited his willingness to take shortcuts to money.

The only good thing I can think of, I guess, is that I also inherited his quiet determination and refusal to be pushed around. Something that ensured I would fight D.J. and his friends as long as it took for them to quit or for me to be so battered and broken I couldn't stand and fight any longer.

Given D.J.'s lack of intelligence, however, from the first day as a freshman at Macon High, I was willing to bet I could get him to quit before me. Except, precisely because of his lack of intelligence, I didn't expect he would learn easily or quickly that he shouldn't mess with Hale or me.

In fact, it took D.J. and his friends only until the day after the chemistry lab attack to try to pay us back for the payback we'd given them. They caught Hale and me in the high school cafeteria during the noon break. Where, naturally, Hale and I sat alone.

■   ■   ■

"Ever eat turtle?" Hale said to me that day in our freshman year.

He didn't give me a chance to answer. Not that I would have. I took his question as rhetorical.

"It ain't bad," he said. "What's interesting is it's got your four basic meat groups."

Four basic *food* groups, I was tempted to say in correction. But this wasn't a conversation I wanted to encourage.

"Part of it's white and tastes like chicken," he said, then proceeded to show he truly did mean the four basic *meat* groups. "Part of it's dark and tastes like beef. Part real fishy-tasting. And the last part, well, it's pure turtle. If you ain't had turtle before, there's no sense trying to explain what it's like. Maybe the way earthworms would taste, but I ain't never had earthworm. Caterpillar, but only once and it was by accident. Had a salad of turnip greens and after one big mouthful, I looked down and there it was. Half a caterpillar, wiggling its green guts in all directions."

I'd been in the process of trying to identify the source of gray gristle buried beneath lumpy gravy. But upon hearing Hale's description, I let the stringy piece of meat slide from my fork and back into the primordial ooze on my plate.

"Not hungry?" he said.

I shook my head.

He took my plate and I didn't protest.

With a mouthful of food, he mumbled, "Best look smart, friend."

That was at the approach of D.J. Johnson and his buddies. D.J.'s shoulders looked far too large and far too ominously powerful in his jean jacket. He didn't waste any time in pleasant conversation. He stopped beside me and yanked up on my collar, pulling me off my chair.

All clattering of tableware in the cafeteria ceased.

Swinging hard, he punched me in the stomach.

I heaved for breath, shocked by the suddenness of the blow, and heard the scrambling of feet. I didn't fight back. It would have been useless. I just hoped somebody was already on the way to get a teacher or the principal.

"That's for yesterday's stunt," he said.

"Because y'all were screaming and crying like a baby?" Hale suggested. "Running down the hall like someone skinned alive? That was pitiful, if you ask me. Big fella like you, making all that noise."

Seeing the sudden puce of anger on D.J.'s face, I knew we were in trouble. I wanted to say a sarcastic thanks to Hale, but I couldn't inhale or exhale. D. J. drew his fist back again.

"After all, it was only salt water," Hale said.

Curiosity triumphed over D.J.'s anger. He held his fist back. "It was acid," D.J. said. "Burned my eyes. If I hadn't washed it off my face fast enough—"

"Salt water," Hale drawled. "Ask Tyrone. He'll explain better than I can. Something about ions and chemical reactions."

Any other time I would have loved explaining the beauty and simplicity of the result of mixing sodium hydroxide and hydrochloric acid. Separately

each was extremely corrosive, because the sodium—
Na—in one and the chlorine—Cl—in the other were
highly reactive elements. But combined, the sodium
atoms attached to the chlorine atoms to form $NaCl$.
Salt. The leftover hydrogen and oxygen combined
to form H_2O. In other words, mixed in the right pro-
portions, sodium hydroxide and hydrochloric acid
produced ordinary salt water. That's what had stung
D.J.'s eyes and fooled him into thinking acid was
eating his face.

"Salt water," Hale repeated with great satisfaction, apparently unaware of how close D.J. was to
a total meltdown. "And you're a moron for crying
about it."

D.J. tensed his fist again.

Hale stood. "That's enough," he growled. "Let him
go. Or I'll have to go after you with my Kentucky
boxing gloves."

If the cafeteria had been silent before, now it
was a total vacuum. In the far corner, someone
cleared a throat. The sound seemed to echo like
distant thunder.

"D.J. Johnson," Principal Wilcox bellowed,
"what is going on here?"

D.J. froze and turned toward her, his fist still
clenched. "I . . . I . . . ," he began to explain. Then,
at a speed that few could match, given his great athletic prowess, he fled through the cafeteria doors,
leaving Principal Wilcox no choice but to follow.

"Well," Hale said, "that couldn't have gone much
better than it did." He put a hand on my shoulder.
"I'm really starting to like you."

"Kentucky boxing gloves?" I asked. "What are those?"

"Switchblades," he explained. "Weapon of choice back where I come from. But I'm really starting to think I won't need them around you."

Because Macon High was a relatively small school, it wasn't difficult to make the football team. All it took was penciling your name on the sign-up sheet. While neither of us thought of ourselves as jocks, Hale and I took advantage of this.

After all, we were both at the age where we were highly aware of girls.

For that matter, Hale was aware of every girl who walked past him. "Hey," he always said with an unapologetic shrug, "perfume is perfume."

As for me, I was a one-woman man. The only trouble was that Kyra James had no awareness of my devotion to her. And, from what it seemed, little awareness that I even existed, aside from my fleeting moment of fame as a wedgied art-deco

piece on the wall in the English room on the first
day of high school.

Either way Hale and I had plenty of incentive to
attempt to impress the opposite sex by pursuing the
glories of football. Or, more importantly, by obtain-
ing a football jacket. We signed up for the team as
soon as the sheet was posted in the gym.

Since I'd played a lot of soccer in Chicago, and
by default—mainly because of my lack of size—
the coach told me to try some field goals. I was as
surprised as anyone when it turned out I had some
natural talent for it.

Hale? He was fast, wiry, and mean. He became
a wide receiver. With the ball in his hands, he was
slippery. When it looked like he couldn't avoid a
tackle, he enjoyed lowering his head and trying to
spear his opponent with his helmet. He too was a
surprise.

Our contributions to the football team could have
ended the enmity that existed between Hale and me
and the jocks, except Hale's attitude was that anything worth taking seriously was worth making
fun of. He truly didn't care about his potential as a
wide receiver. This, as much as his flippant attitude,
infuriated the Macon jocks, who spent their school
careers measuring themselves by their athletic status.

Of course diplomatic relations were also strained
by the fact that D.J. still wanted very badly to
hurt us.

He didn't, because on the first day of football
practice, I had promised him if he hurt Hale or me
in any way, if he didn't do his utmost to protect us

on and off the football field, I would find other ways
to chemically alter his life.

And I didn't mean by drug-induced euphoria.

He knew that and was truly afraid of us.

I guess, then, it was because of D.J. that I became
friends with Hale, and because of D.J. that Hale and I
met Sammy James the way we did, back in our freshman year.

■   ■   ■

About three weeks after the day I'd been hung by
my shorts on a coat hook and from that painful
perspective first saw and fell in love with his twin
sister, Kyra, Sammy approached us in the high
school cafeteria. It was noon.

Hale and I sat alone, a custom established from
our first days at Macon High.

"I ever tell you about my aunt Freda?" Hale
asked.

I removed my gaze from Kyra James, who sat
with Miranda Sanchez at the opposite end of the
cafeteria, and popped a fry into my mouth.

I didn't need to answer Hale's question. Hale, I'd
learned, had an endless supply of family stories, par-
tially because it seemed he had an endless extended
family—one that populated a large part of Hazard
County in the Appalachian Mountains of southeast
Kentucky. The bulk of them shared the Ramsey sur-
name. I'd also learned that when Hale had a family
story to tell, he started with a question to establish I
had not heard it before. I didn't know yet whether to

believe the tales of his family back in the hills, but they were entertaining. And they took my mind off the deep and unrequited yearning I had for a girl named Kyra James.

"No one could figure out why Freda took a job at the local veterinarian," Hale began with his thick twang. "But we weren't surprised when she quit after a week or two. Freda wasn't much for work. Seemed she saved up just enough to buy a life insurance policy for Uncle Leroy."

"Uh-huh," I said absently. Even fluorescent light looked good as it bounced off Kyra's hair. I knew someone like her would never date someone like me, but I still couldn't take my eyes off her.

"Let me ask you something," Hale said. "If you had a choice of paying 10 dollars for a flu shot at the doctor's office, or letting your wife give you one, what would you take?"

That snapped me to attention. "Huh?"

Hale grinned. "Exactly. She announced she was going to save Leroy some money. He said he hadn't even figured on getting a flu shot, so she wasn't really saving him a thing, but she told him to drop his drawers and get ready. Then she pulled out a needle . . ."

Hale held his hands apart as if showing me the length of a fish he'd caught. "This long. Horse needle. My cousin Abe said Leroy jumped a country mile when she jabbed him with it. And by the time he landed, he was out like she'd whacked him with a log."

I studied Hale's face to see if he was stringing me along.

He lifted his hands in protest. "Truth," he said. "I couldn't make this up if I wanted. Turned out Freda had stolen the needle from the vet. Along with the stuff they use to put dogs to sleep. She'd pumped ol' Leroy with enough to kill a horse."

"And . . . your point is . . ."

Hale snorted. "He's a Ramsey. Takes a lot more than that to get rid of one of us. There was this time he—"

Hale stopped. Looked over my shoulder.

I shifted.

Sammy James was five steps away, approaching our table.

He was a big guy. Quiet, reserved. Didn't seem to be part of any group at Macon High, although he played sports. Had left us alone when the jocks tormented us. Didn't protect us. Didn't join in. Just stayed on the sidelines.

"Mind if I join you?" he asked.

I shrugged.

Hale shrugged.

Sammy spun a chair backward and sat. "I've been sent by a delegation," he said, grinning.

"Delegation?" I echoed. "What delegation?"

"Let me put it this way," he continued. "D.J. has a new respect for the powers of science."

"Oh," I said. "The jocks."

"They are all terrified of what you might do next," Sammy said. "They want a truce."

"Truce," Hale repeated.

"Truce," Sammy confirmed. "It was the gangrene thing on the face and arms that scared them the most." He shook his head in admiration. "How exactly did you pull that off?"

"We neither confirm nor deny responsibility for that," I said, keeping a straight face. It was silver nitrate, but I wasn't prepared to reveal the secrets of chemical wizardry behind it.

Silver nitrate comes in a powder, readily obtainable by mail order, which was how I got most of my supplies. It will do no damage to the human body. But upon contact with skin it turns the skin a blackish purple that cannot be washed off. It takes days for it to disappear.

As I'd explained to Hale, say you left your lunch bag in a place where a person could steal your sandwich. Say every day when you opened it, you discovered exactly that. All you'd have to do is put some silver nitrate on the bread, and wherever that person handled your sandwich, his or her fingers would become blackish purple. The silver nitrate in that situation would be a marker, no different that the exploding dyes that banks put in bags of money to foil banker robbers.

Hale had said, "Great idea. Except that since we just had lunch in the cafeteria, we don't have sandwiches to steal." Then he'd observed, "But what good will it do if the jocks actually do steal the sandwiches and get purple-black fingers? After all, it's no secret that they're in a war with us."

I'd pointed out to Hale that the athletic department had a laundry room where all the jerseys were washed after football practice. It probably wouldn't be difficult to sneak in after hours and apply silver nitrate to anything that came out of the dryer. And that whatever we applied it to would be placed in their lockers the next morning, to be ready for practice in the afternoon.

"Practice jerseys," Hale had said with a snort. "That isn't much of a way to pay them back."

Again he was right.

But his assumption was wrong.

We didn't apply silver nitrate to their jerseys.

But to their towels.

After showering and drying, all the jocks looked like blackened victims of gangrene. Most had panicked and gone to a doctor. All had remained blackened for at least a week.

I'd promised D.J. there were plenty more tricks to come if the war didn't stop. That Sammy was now sitting in front of us proved D.J. had believed me.

"What do you say?" Sammy asked. "They'll promise to leave you alone if you promise to leave them alone."

"On one condition," Hale said.

I raised my eyebrows. I would have been happy enough with a simple truce.

"I want an apology," Hale continued.

Sammy crossed his arms and leaned forward, resting on the back of the chair. "Might be tough. Then they're going to want apologies. I mean, let's face it. You've done as much damage to them as they have to you. I'd say if you added it up, it's even Steven."

"Nope." Hale stuck to his guns. "They started it. All we've done is pay them back each time."

"I'll give you that," Sammy said. "But I don't understand what you're getting at."

"Simple," Hale replied. "We don't want an apology for any of the times they beat us up. That was payback for payback. But it never would have started if D.J. hadn't hung us up on coat hooks our first day here."

"So that's what you want. Apologies for that."

"Public apologies. In front of the same class that saw us up on the coat hooks."

Sammy smiled. It was an easy, likable smile from an easy, likable guy.

"I think," he said, "that they are desperate enough to agree to that." He stood and extended his right hand. "Deal?"

"Deal," Hale said, shaking hands.

"Deal," I said, shaking hands.

Sammy grinned at me. "Come on, how'd you do it?"

I just smiled. "Secrets of the trade."

He smiled back. "Figured. Just like a magician. But it wasn't going to hurt to ask."

That's how our first meeting ended.

I kept those secrets until my first date with Kyra, halfway through my senior year.

And, looking back, that day, Friday, December 31, was the beginning of the events that led to Sammy's death.

New Year's Eve. This was the night for the date I'd been waiting for since hanging on a coat hook by my underwear on my first day at Macon High. The day that I was looking down at Kyra James, the blonde goddess, with such longing that most of the humiliation at the hands of D.J. Johnson was pushed aside.

After saying good-bye to Sammy, Kyra and I had just stepped outside of her house. It was only two blocks from Gran's apartment, but until that night when I finally had her permission to visit, a universe away. We were on our way to a New Year's Eve party at the local Holiday Inn. I still couldn't believe my dream girl had finally agreed to go out with me.

I'd splurged and bought two tickets to a gala there, hoping that taking her to a real party with waiters in tuxedos and champagne served in flute glasses might impress her more than trying to find a party of high school kids that would be loud and noisy.

All right, the truth is nobody would ever invite me to a high school party that was worth going to. And if we did go, I knew there'd be a bunch of cool guys making moves on Kyra and she'd forget about me.

So a party at a Holiday Inn—with Hale and his date there too—seemed like the best possible solution. Of course, the tickets hadn't been cheap. But that should always impress a girl, even if all the old people around would dance like the living dead.

At Kyra's house, I'd hardly been able to breathe, seeing Kyra walk down the stairs as I joked with Sammy. She wore a long, dark dress that made her seem incredibly grown-up. I'd helped her into her coat, absorbing her wonderful perfume. Then I'd stuttered good-bye to Sammy and her parents and escorted her down the steps.

A cool guy would have had a car.

Not me. I'd been saving what money I could, but I still didn't have enough.

Fortunately, I'd also picked the party on basis of location. Only a couple blocks farther, closer to the downtown of Macon.

And that's when I'd looked up at the winter sky uncluttered with clouds and had said the stupid comment about the stars.

"Stars are cool," I said, pointing upward. I felt like I'd burst with this strange emotion that had never filled me before. Kyra James! With me! I wanted to impress her and dance with her and sing to her and swim across an ocean with her. All at the same time. It didn't make sense, I know, but neither did this bubbly feeling inside. "Millions and millions of miles across. The force of gravity at the center of a star ignites the hydrogen atoms. Well, not ignites. Fuses them together on a nuclear level. Here on Earth we produce energy in atomic bombs by splitting the atoms. Stars actually compress them."

Her responding silence made me believe she was actually considering the intertwining of physics and chemistry.

"Think of it this way," I said, still serious and enthusiastic. "All of the energy in this universe is created by gravity, the weakest force known to physics, and still nobody can explain why or how gravity works the way it does. Cool, huh?"

"Wow," she said. "And here I thought the stars were all about poetry and romance."

"Um, yeah." I kicked at a piece of frozen grass. "Suppose that means you don't want to discuss light-years and how much time it takes for that romantic starlight to reach the Earth, huh?"

She giggled. That was encouraging.

We walked. I moved briskly because the air was chilly.

"Hey, brainiac," she called. From behind me. "I'm on high heels."

Oops.

I stopped. She caught up. Because she was on high heels, did it mean she was afraid of falling?

Had she told me that because she wanted to hold hands?

With my right hand I poked the air in her direction.

She probably didn't get the hint, because she put her hands in her pockets.

"Hey," Kyra said. The glow from a streetlight behind her made a halo around her head. Wow, she was beautiful. "Speaking of brainiacs, are you ever going to let anyone in on your wizardry secrets?"

"Wizardry secrets."

"You know, like what you did to the jocks in your freshman year so they finally left you alone?"

"I didn't know you knew about that."

"Come on. Sammy's my brother. Of course he told me how he had to approach you and Hale to make the peace deal. Only he never told me exactly what you did."

"I don't know . . ."

"Come on." She took my hand and walked with me. "Tell, tell, tell."

We were a half block away from the Holiday Inn. Christmas lights sparkled in all directions. Kyra James was holding my hand!

"Silver nitrate," I said and explained.

By the time I finished, we were nearly at the Holiday Inn. She laughed so hard, she slipped on some ice at the entrance.

"Tyrone Larson," she said, grabbing me, "you're a genius."

She was still holding on to me from where she'd grabbed my shoulders when she'd nearly fallen. Her beautiful face was only inches away. I wanted to kiss her. But didn't dare. I just sighed with happiness.

"Kyra," I said, "I'm so glad we're going on a date."

She smiled and took my arm.

"Since freshman year," I said, "I've been hoping and hoping and waiting my turn. And finally, tonight. It was sure worth the wait."

She straightened.

The main door to the Holiday Inn was only three steps away. Other couples passed us. Couples coming from cars in the parking lot. Not couples who were walking because the guy on the date didn't have a car.

"What did you say?" she said.

"It was sure worth the wait. Thank you."

"No. Before that. Something about waiting your turn."

"Yeah," I said, unaware of the storm about to hit. "You've dated just about all the guys at the high school. I was hoping I'd make your list."

"All the guys." Her voice was as cold as the air. "My list."

"Um . . ."

"What exactly are you saying about me?" she said. Still cold.

"That you're beautiful and I'm happy to get my chance."

"That's what I am. A chance. Like you're just one more guy ready to spin the wheel."

"No, no," I said. "It's not like that."

"You make me sound very cheap, Tyrone Larson."

"No. No." Why was I wrecking this evening? "It's not like that."

"Suddenly, I don't feel much like being with you in public. I'd hate to give people the wrong impression. Especially those who keep count of who I date and who I don't date."

"Kyra . . ."

"I'll find my own way home."

"Stop," I said. Desperate. "Am I wrong?"

"Yes, you're wrong. I'm not that kind of girl."

"I mean about the guys you've dated. Except for me and D.J. Johnson, who haven't you gone out with at least once?"

"None of your business." She backed away from me.

"I think I know why."

She glared at me. But didn't take another step away.

"It's because nobody's quite the right person for you," I said. I had given this a lot of thought. Mainly because I'd given the subject of Kyra a lot of thought. "I think it would take somebody amazing. Somebody who has everything. Smart. Nice. Funny. Good athlete. Maybe somebody with just enough mystery to keep you interested. And there's no one like that in our high school."

The hardness of her face softened somewhat. She was a gorgeous statue, this tall girl wrapped in an overcoat, with her blonde hair slowly moving in the night wind.

"So it's like you're nice enough to give each of us a chance." I stared at the ground. "I really didn't think I'd be the one. But I have always wished I would be. You know, like the ugly duckling that . . ." I stopped and looked up. "Forget I said anything. Just forget it. I'm not the one for you, no matter how much I wish I was."

If this were a movie, this would have been the moment. When her eyes were opened to who I was. And she suddenly realized I was the right guy for her.

Instead, a couple of college-age guys walked out of the Holiday Inn. Tough guys. With no jackets. Wearing just T-shirts and jeans. One of them held a can of beer.

"Hey, baby!" the closest one said to Kyra. "If I told you that you had a great body, would you hold it against me?"

His friend cackled.

I turned to them. "Shut up."

"Oooh, what's the little man going to do?" the second one said. He staggered against his buddy.

"Just shut up."

The first one laughed. "Dude, if you're looking to fight, this is not the right time. It's not like you're going to impress anyone."

He pointed.

I turned.

Kyra, fleeing, had already reached the street.

I ran to catch up to her.

"Go away," she said. "Just go away. I don't like men right now. And I don't like you. Go away. Please."

I did.

Unaware that the catalyst named Mitchell Wade

had already entered Macon and would be waiting for all of us—Kyra, me, Sammy, Hale, Miranda, Brianna—when school started at the beginning of the new year.

Monday, three days later.

"You and I are about to change, to alter one another's lives for all time. We only have one semester, so we better get started."

This was Mitchell Wade's prophetic statement, the one that would echo through my mind a few months later as I sat in a room in a police station waiting for Detective Sanders to grill me. *"You and I are about to change, to alter one another's lives for all time. We only have one semester, so we better get started."*

A minute before he said it, Mitchell Wade had walked into the classroom, half sat and half leaned against his desk, and surveyed all of us.

I'd only looked up because the murmuring around me had drawn me from my thoughts about sneezing. A few seconds earlier, I'd sneezed. Into a tissue of course.

Naturally, that had led me into thinking about how dangerous it is to hold in a sneeze. You know, when it's supposed to be real quiet and you get that itchy feeling in your nose that tells you that it's on its way and there's no stopping it.

Sneezus interruptus is not smart, however. A good sneeze fires airborne particles at about 100 feet a second, nearly 70 miles an hour. That's because your body is trying to clear out debris like pollen or dirt from your sinuses and needs all that force.

When you hold the sneeze, it reverses all the tremendous force inward. Instead of a satisfying explosion, you get an implosion. One that can cause fractures in the cartilage of your nose. Or burst your eardrums. Break blood vessels in your eyes. Detach your retina. Seriously. It can even cause a fatal stroke. I mean, there should be public-health posters warning people about all these things. But there aren't. And did I mention that if you hold in a sneeze when you're sick, you can actually drive the millions of infected particles that your body is trying to get rid of right back into your sinus tissues? And you could get a ghastly infection?

There I was, wondering if a person could apply for a government grant to design a health poster to warn people against this horrible danger, when the murmuring around me grew and grew.

When I glanced up, I saw the reason for the murmuring.

Mitchell Wade was a tanned handsome guy in

a sports jacket and a brown turtleneck sweater. A tanned handsome guy young enough to look like he still belonged in college. Tanned? In the middle of an Iowa winter?

I'd first figured him for a substitute since Mrs. Overstreet had not shown up for class. But most substitute teachers are afraid of high school kids. He was not. Just surveyed us like he was royalty and we were an audience in a hick town.

Minutes later our principal, Mrs. Wilcox, stepped into the room and announced that Mrs. Overstreet had suffered a slight stroke. The school had been fortunate enough to hire Mr. Mitchell Wade. Would we all welcome him?

After all the girls—and I mean all—applauded, he walked to the window and stared at the snow-covered parking lot. He let the silence build, then flipped around to face us and spoke.

"So this is Iowa."

Like we were blessed to have him in our presence.

And then the partial lie and partial truth and partial prophecy that set everything in motion: "You and I are about to change, to alter one another's lives for all time. We only have one semester, so we better get started."

At first it wasn't much of a threat. Getting started consisted of going through the class list and, one by one, calling each of us by name.

But that was only his warm-up.

In less than 10 minutes, he'd established himself. Charismatic. Charming. Poised. Likable. Especially to the girls, who seemed to giggle at everything he said. He was everything my own father was not.

He told us he came from California and then made some jokes about breaking up with his old girlfriend. The girls giggled again at that. But the guys in the class just raised their eyebrows. I think we all instinctively knew he was making a between-the-lines statement: *Yeah, guys, I'm young. But don't mess with me. I can lose a person and laugh about it. Replace someone easily. And you high school guys are lucky if you own a 10-year-old car and can find a date who will let you hold hands.*

After a while I started to tune the banter out of my head. Until he pulled out a baseball and started to throw it around the room, asking everyone to give him one of their New Year's resolutions before toss-ing the ball back to him. Some of the kids tried play-ing it safe, but Mitchell Wade busted them good.

Then it was my turn.

After he threw me the ball, I waited until my silence forced him to repeat his instructions. "Give us your New Year's resolution and throw the ball back."

"Do my best," I finally said, trying to appear uninterested in his game. That was my niche here at Macon High. I wasn't cool or anything, just in my own little world. And I liked it that way. "That's about it," I concluded.

Then I stupidly played into his game by firing the ball back harder than it came. Not only did he catch it, he grinned. "Only the mediocre are at their best, Tyrone."

There were *ooh*s all around the room, as if he'd just won that round too. I thought of an easy comeback to knock him off his perch. *Yeah, like Michael Jordan and Tiger Woods. Were they mediocre at their best? Hardly.*

But even if I'd been willing to actually talk back to Mitchell Wade, I wouldn't have gotten the chance. He'd already thrown the ball to someone else.

tyrone's story

Soon after his arrival at Macon High, something strange happened with attendance in Mitch Wade's English class. Fewer students were skipping than before, when Mrs. Overstreet taught. They weren't waiting in the hallway until the last possible minute to go inside the classroom. And the girls were filling the front seats instead of hanging with the guys in the back.

I knew this because of Kyra and the fact that I was generally so aware of her presence.

She'd gone to New York with her parents to visit NYU, the university she would be attending after high school, which in itself was a big deal. The fact that the James family all went ahead of time, to check out the school, was impressive enough. Even more so was the fact that someone from Macon, Iowa, was clearly destined for bright lights and big city.

While Kyra was gone in New York, I felt like I was walking around beneath a personal rain cloud. I was glad to see her back at Macon High, even if she was ignoring me as usual.

I also noticed that she and Miranda rushed into the first-period English class the day she was back at school, both trying not to look like they were rushing in.

This was on Monday, January 9, one week after Mitchell Wade had first introduced himself to us at Macon High.

Just before Kyra's arrival I'd been thinking about yawning. Hale had yawned, which had made me yawn. And then thinking about it had triggered another yawn.

I'll do that once in a while—talk to someone else about it just to time how long it takes to make them yawn. It's an experiment I've done a dozen times. See, I tell the person that yawning is not a way for the body to get rid of carbon dioxide like you might have been told. Nope. Scientists have done experiments to show that a person in an oxygen chamber yawns as much as anyone else. That's the kind of job I'd like. Getting paid to answer questions like that. Which, of course, has nothing to do with why we yawn. I'd give you the answer, but no one really knows. The best guess is that somehow it's meant to synchronize clan behavior, because humans are the only animals who yawn. At the very least it's fun to discuss, just to watch the other person yawn.

I'd yawned three times, waiting for class to begin, cutting my last yawn short when Kyra walked in. Her presence was always powerful enough to take me away from my weird thoughts and digressions, thoughts I did not inflict on her and Miranda as they entered the classroom.

Both of them scanned the front rows of desks for a spot, when usually both headed right away to the back. This time neither could find a place to sit.

Was it coincidence that the front rows were all girls? I doubt it, not with Mitchell Wade as the teacher.

Tressa, a red-haired cheerleader, smiled with triumph. "Tried to save you a seat, Kyra," Tressa said with a fake smile, smoothing her short skirt down over her legs.

Saving a seat? That told me plenty. Never before had I seen any students save seats for other students in a classroom situation.

Kyra's fake smile to Tressa in return also told me plenty, as if she knew that Tressa knew that each was faking her smile to the other.

So Miranda and Kyra wandered to the back. Their perfume filled the air. Hale, beside me, inhaled deeply and grinned. I elbowed Hale.

Moments later Mitchell Wade made his entrance. This too I studied, on the chance I could learn something from it. Mr. Wade sat on his desk, not behind it.

"I want us to talk about something really important today," Mr. Wade said, his eyes making it seem as if he were staring into the soul of every one of us. Then he jumped up and slammed a textbook shut. Tony, the kid it belonged to, jumped in his seat. In the shocked silence of that moment, Mr. Wade said, "Forget the books. This semester we're going to learn more from life."

Looking back, I realize I should have paid more attention to that statement. Like many of the things he said, it was an eerie prophecy.

A couple students agreed with Mr. Wade.

"What a cool dude," Hale whispered to me. "Glad he did that. I was ready to spitball Tony."

Mr. Wade had now moved away from the desk. "Will someone tell me what beauty is?" he asked.

In my book, all a person had to do was look at Kyra. But she wasn't making any moves to answer the question.

Instead, Brianna, her rival, stood up and bowed.

We laughed. Except for Hale. He applauded.

Mr. Wade laughed too, and the discussion moved forward. Point by point he began to develop his argument that opinions and morals differ from one person to the next. Who was to say that one person was right over another?

Taylor, a girl jock and friend of Miranda's, raised her hand when Mr. Wade brought the argument to that point. "If we get our morals from God and our facts from the Bible," she said, "then right and wrong have a factual basis. They're not opinions."

"But what if I don't believe in your God, in your particular right and wrong?" Mr. Wade fired back. His smile was patronizing, as if he already knew how to trump her answer.

I admired Taylor for smiling right back. "Facts are

true whether you believe them or not, aren't they? You might not believe there's an Empire State Building, but it doesn't mean the building doesn't exist."

"Ah," Mr. Wade said. It was obvious that he was enjoying this. "But you could show someone photos of the Empire State Building. Or take them there. There are any number of ways to show the evidence of its existence. You can't, however, say that about God."

I couldn't help myself. I put up my hand. Even if I didn't believe in God, I couldn't stand to see anyone misrepresent science or scientific theories. It was just another of the weird things about me.

Mr. Wade clutched his chest, faking a heart attack. "Tyrone? You? Actually speaking in class?" Then he grinned to show he didn't mean it as an insult.

"Well," I said, "actually there's a lot of scientific evidence for the existence of God."

There were a few groans. "Come on, Ty," Jamal said. "This is English lit. No science, please."

I shrugged. If no one wanted to hear me, that was fine. I'd go back to keeping my mouth shut.

"No," Mr. Wade said. "This is a wide-ranging discussion on the relativity of values, and I'm intrigued by what Ty has to say. After all, if there is proof that God exists, then what Taylor says has some merit. Ty?"

"The anthropic principle," I said. "In essence, a growing number of respected scientists believe the sole purpose of the universe is to produce human life."

"Go on," Mr. Wade said.

I couldn't help myself, or my enthusiasm. The words seemed to tumble out of me. "Gravity, electromagnetism, the weak nuclear force, and the strong nuclear force. These are the four fundamental forces of the universe. Scientists have run programs on supercomputers to see what the universe would be like if any of the four were changed even slightly. I mean, changes of less than a twentieth of a percentage point. And they were surprised to find out that the only way the universe can support life is the way it was designed. Then they started noticing other coincidences about physics. Every one made life possible."

"But it could happen by chance," Mr. Wade said. "Just like I could win a lottery."

"If you won the lottery 50 weeks in a row," I answered, "would that be chance, or would that be rigged?"

"I'd be in jail," Mr. Wade admitted. "So would the person who helped me win all 50 times."

"Well," I said, ignoring a flashback to my father and how he was in jail because of what he'd rigged with the finances at his charity organization, "that's why so many scientists are blown away. The random chance of everything being just perfect to support life is the same as winning the lottery 50 times in a row. Mathematically impossible. Many are prepared to conclude the universe was designed."

Taylor gave me a grateful smile, as if I'd said what I did to help her. But I hadn't. It's just because I believe in the importance of truth and the pursuit of truth. I wasn't about to try to get to know God or anything. I'd seen my own dad fail at that. But it didn't mean I had to pretend God didn't exist.

"Point well taken, Ty," Mr. Wade said. "But does acknowledgment of the existence of God allow us to understand the nature of God?"

I thought about that. "No," I finally answered.

"So you would agree that even if a super being created the universe, there can be relative good and relative evil within it?"

I thought again, aware that all eyes were on me. I shook my head. Because of the bad example of my father, I wasn't big on religion. But as a person interested in science, yes, I was committed to trying to understand truth.

"Hitler," I said. "What he did to try to exterminate the Jews in World War II was absolutely evil by any standards. Will you agree with me on that?"

Mr. Wade nodded. "And your point?"

"You've agreed on one example that we've defined as absolute evil. If I find you one example of absolute evil, then absolute evil exists. Just like if you found me one photo of the Empire State Building, I would be forced to admit it exists. And if absolute evil does exist, then relative evil can't exist. Because it's one or the other, and simple reasoning has eliminated one of them. And if absolute evil can exist, then its counterpart, absolute good, must also exist. Therefore . . ."

Mr. Wade was applauding me. Actually applauding me.

"Come on, guys," Mr. Wade said to the rest of the

class. "That was impressive. Really impressive. I'm going to admit in front of all of you that Ty has given me something very profound to think about."

I was just as surprised when the rest of the class joined in the applause.

I snuck a look over at Kyra to see if I'd impressed her, but the expression on her face was distant, as if her thoughts had taken her to another galaxy.

"Come by my bike shop after school, Ty," Mr. Wade said, breaking into my thoughts. "Love to have you as part of our club."

All right, I thought. I just might do that.

Especially when, right after class, Mr. Wade drew me aside. "Of all the guys in the class," he said, "I think you're the most like me. We don't care what other people think."

"You're right," I said and grinned.

I was impressed at the way Mr. Wade talked straight to me, man to man. I didn't know then how much I needed that, especially with having a father in prison. But later I was to find out how much Mr. Wade's charisma had drawn me in—and Sammy too. I even began to think of him as "Mitch"—instead of "Mr. Wade."

"Tyrone," Mitch said. "Hale. Good to see you both. Sam and I have an important question for you."

It was after school that same day. Hale and I had just walked into Mitch's bike shop. It was on Main Street, with a doughnut shop on one side and a car-repair shop on the other. The front of the bike shop had great-looking mountain bikes with price tags that ranged from a couple hundred to a couple thousand dollars. Posters of bike races lined the walls. Other gear was scattered, but in such a way that made the interior look hip.

I'd heard people around town—adults in coffee shops mainly—laugh at Mitch's bike shop. Setting it up in winter, they'd scoffed, how could it possibly do any business? "Fancy California stuff," others

said. "That's not what works here in the Midwest."
And so on and so on.

But people shut up when they saw that Mitch had
actually organized a team that did training runs in
the winter. If it wasn't snowing or the roads weren't
icy, the bikers went out.

And it looked like Mitch was selling bikes too.
A couple of lawyers and doctors had taken some
of the high-end bikes, going around town in sleek
biking outfits and waving cheerily at anyone who
honked at them.

In all, I wasn't surprised. Mitch had that kind of
effect on people. And now he was scrutinizing Hale
and me, as if how we answered would change world
history.

"It's about women," Mitch said. "Sammy here
thinks he needs to be more interesting and more
like a party animal to get their attention. Have any
suggestions on how to understand them?"

"Absolutely none," Hale drawled. "They're the
most bewitching creatures on this planet."

"Ty?" Mitch asked. "You did pretty well in class
earlier with your arguments about God and science
and relative good and evil. Surely the subject of
women is much easier for a brain like you."

"I charge an hourly consulting rate," I said.
"I doubt any of you can afford it."

Sammy laughed. Which was the result I wanted.
I was utterly in love with his sister. No way was
I going to let any of these guys into my head on
this subject.

"See," Sammy said. "I need to be funny. Or something. Anything so she doesn't think I'm just some boring nice guy. Girls don't like boring nice guys."

"Guess he might have to find a way to raise the money for your consulting fee," Mitch said to me, grinning. "Sam here has got it bad. He's not naming names, though. Just wants advice."

He didn't have to name names. It was obvious. It was Miranda. One of his sister's best friends.

My head spun over Kyra.

Sammy's over Miranda.

And Hale over Brianna.

It was Mitch who needed to give all of us advice. I told him so. Without naming names.

"Well," Mitch said, "here's one thing to remember. After a quarrel between a man and a woman, the man feels bad mainly from thinking he might have hurt the woman, but a woman feels bad mainly from thinking she didn't hurt the man badly enough."

Hale snorted. "Cold, man. Real cold."

"Actually, that wasn't me. That was a paraphrase of a quote by a philosopher named Friedrich Nietzsche. He was also the one to say that love is a state where a man sees things most decidedly as they are not."

Love is a state where a man sees things most decidedly as they are not. I should have latched onto that, held it, examined it, and remembered it for the next few months. But I was laughing and basking too much in the presence of someone as cool as Mitchell Wade, who could quote philosophers as easily as if he were reading basketball scores from the newspaper.

"Actually, I can't say I'm the person to offer advice," Mitch continued. "And it's an age-old question, man versus woman. I do know, however, that if you're too anxious and you show too much how much you like a woman, she tends to back away."

Hale and I and Sammy nodded, as if we understood.

Behind Mitch, on the workbench, dozens of bike parts were scattered. Obviously Sammy had walked in as Mitch was doing repairs. And Hale and I had done the same, probably only a few minutes later.

"Plus," Mitch said, "it helps to speak their language."

"Language?" Sammy echoed.

"Sure," Mitch said. "Women speak differently than men. They feel a certain way about things. Don't ask them what they think about something, ask them what they feel about something. Then listen. Women love it if you listen."

We all nodded.

"See, when they come to you with a problem, don't offer advice. Because if you do, they'll think you aren't listening. That you don't care. They don't want you to solve the problem for them. They just want you to listen."

We kept nodding.

"So you, for example," Mitch said to me. "If a girl comes to you with a problem, nod sympathetically, agree with her about every two minutes, and in your mind, solve science problems. When she's finished talking, she'll feel like you really care. And in the meanwhile, you haven't really wasted any time, because in your mind, you've gone on a different journey. Got it?"

"Got it." I grinned.

"And when a woman asks you a difficult question that involves feelings," Mitch said, "the smartest thing to do is pause, look thoughtful, and repeat the question right back to them. It does two things. Gives you time to scramble for the right answer and, better yet, allows you to build off the answer she gives you. Most often, just find a way to repeat what she said, saying it differently, and you'll be fine."

Hale offered Mitch a high five. Mitch took it, grinning.

"More seriously though," Mitch added, "there's one thing I wish I'd figured out a lot earlier than I did. Women are real people. Not images or goddesses or objects. Please, please remember that."

"Sure," Hale said. "Real people. Except mysterious and so good-looking they make your head spin."

Mitch sighed. "Enough of this for one day. You guys ready to go on a bike run?"

"Not me," Hale scoffed. "I've got 300 horses to take me wherever I want."

"Your Camaro, huh," Mitch replied. "I've seen you around town in it. Probably do a good job of leaving my Porsche in the dust."

Mitch couldn't have said anything better to make Hale beam with pride.

"You, Ty?"

"Don't like sweat," I said. "The chemical composition of it is dangerously close to urea."

Sammy made a face.

"Sammy?" Mitch asked.

"Got too much homework," he said. "I'm really struggling with my physics and chemistry right now."

Mitch looked at me. "Ty? Can you help him? I've heard you're the man when it comes to stuff like that."

Usually I didn't offer help to anyone. But with Mitch right there, I felt it was the right thing to do. Plus it was a way to be around Kyra, if the timing was right and she was at home the same time Sammy was.

I turned toward Sammy. "I'd be glad to help. If you want."

"I want," he said eagerly. "If I don't get this stuff down, I'll never make it to college. Wouldn't want that. Not with a twin sister who nails everything perfectly."

"That's settled then," Mitch said. "Where are you guys going to meet and when?"

"Doughnut shop," Sammy suggested. "Tonight after supper. Don't want my sister knowing that I need help with physics when she doesn't."

So much for my hope that I'd be able to spend time in the same house as Kyra.

"Sounds good" is all I said.

Sammy grabbed his book bag, gave us a wave, and headed out the front door.

Mitch surveyed Hale and me. "Guys, I think I have something that might interest you. A piece of the profits of MLM."

"MLM," Hale repeated.

"Multilevel marketing."

"Like Amway," I suggested.

"In a way. But it's vitamins, health supplements, and diet stuff. From my California connections. It's a good living." Mitch grinned. "My Porsche is proof of that. It's not a Camaro, but not everyone can be Hale."

Hale grinned too.

Mitch got serious. "Here's the deal." His voice dropped. "I'm making so much money with it that I've had to look for a way to hide it from the Infernal Revenue Service. Since I've moved here, I've been getting it shipped to Des Moines by bus. Under a different name. With me so far?"

Hale nodded. I listened.

"Anyway," Mitch continued, "it'd be great if you guys could make a run to the Greyhound there and pick it up for me. What's it to Des Moines? Forty-five minutes?"

"Can do it in half that time," Hale said.

"Can, but shouldn't," Mitch answered. "I'm not going to pay for your speeding tickets. The real satisfaction is making sure they don't catch you. Drive a careful four or six miles above the speed limit, and you'll never get pulled over. See, play the system, Hale. Like going into the bank for a loan. Wear the right clothes, say the right things, they'll hand you money. It's not joining the system. It's beating it by its own rules. Like this IRS stuff."

Hale nodded again. "Shoot, if it's helping you beat the government, any self-respecting hillbilly will go along for the ride. And I'm both. Self-respecting. And a hillbilly."

Mitch pulled out his wallet. Handed Hale a hundred-dollar bill.

Handed one to me too.

"What do you think?" Mitch said. "Does that cover your gas and time?"

If I could rewind time, that's the moment I would go back and find. Then make a different decision.

But I didn't know then what I know now.

So, stupidly, I took the money.

And Hale and I did make that trip to Des Moines. Hale waited in the Camaro while I ran in to the counter, signed for the package, and brought it back to the car.

It was only the first of many trips that we would make for Mitchell Wade.

(now)

"What wound did ever heal but by degrees?"

Othello, Act II, Scene 3

It's Tuesday. Sammy's been dead for 11 days.

Yesterday I'd been taken out of class and driven to the police station. Barely 24 hours have passed since I left the interrogation at the police station. But it feels much longer than that. Much longer.

When I park my green Escort, Brianna Devereaux is sitting on the steps that lead into my apartment building. I turn off my ignition. From behind my steering wheel, I sit and watch and wonder what she is doing there.

It has started to rain. Part of my mind focuses on that. I hear the patter of raindrops on the clear plastic that I have duct-taped into place where my rear window used to be. I worry about the rain leaking through. I know what mildewed car seats smell like, and it isn't pleasant.

The other part of my mind registers the presence of Brianna. Protected from the rain by the awning above her, she sits with apparent serenity. As if she is a queen surveying her world.

She knows I am watching her because she waves.

I don't bother to wave back.

In fact, I turn on my ignition.

That startles her into moving toward me and gives me satisfaction. Like suddenly she's not in as much control as she believed.

It's a short satisfaction, however. I picture her walking back to the apartment building and going inside, through the cabbage smell that comes from our neighbor's cooking, and knocking on the door. I imagine the look on Gran's face when she recognizes Brianna as the girl that I stayed with all night two and a half weeks ago.

That is not good.

So I don't drive away as I intended. Instead I reach across and unlock the passenger door. Brianna slides in.

Then I drive. I don't want Gran to look out her window and see me parked with Brianna. I wonder who I'm more ashamed of—Brianna or me?

I glance into the rearview mirror, as if to reassure myself that I am out of sight of the apartment. But all I see is the clear plastic I have duct-taped, now sagging with the weight of rainwater. It reminds me of Hale and why he left. It reminds me of my own anger and guilt and self-hatred.

"Hear you went down to the police station," she says. "What did you tell them?"

"And hello and how are you?" I reply, letting sarcasm drip into my voice.

"Pull over," she says.

I ignore her. Now that Gran can't see us, I have no compelling reason to let Brianna tell me what to do.

I am angry at her for what once happened between us. I am angry at myself for having allowed it to happen. It's childish, I know—my pleasure in ignoring her—but I don't care.

"Pull over," she says again, obviously not realizing how much I enjoy irritating her.

As I continue to drive, the car is loud, with the wind that seeps through the plastic sheet and the rain growing harder on the roof.

"Pull over," Brianna says one more time. Now there is nothing soft and fuzzy about her voice. Gone is the teasing quality she likes to add to her tone when she speaks around guys.

So I know she's serious. I pull over.

I park under an oak that is just starting to grow leaves for the spring. The leaves, however, are not enough shelter from the water that is about to seep into my backseat.

"I want you to listen carefully," she says. "I'm afraid that Hale is going to turn both of us in for drugs."

I shake my head. "You're crazy," I tell Brianna.

Hale? Turn me in for drugs? Hale and I are history as friends, I think, but I know he'd never betray me like that. I just don't buy it.

I wonder what Brianna's up to.

"How much time do you want to do in jail?" she asked. "In case you haven't noticed, some serious stuff is coming down. And Hale's going to try to pin it on you. On me."

As Brianna is talking, I'm thinking about Gran back at the apartment. Gran, who will be waiting for me with milk and cookies. She'll be wearing an apron too.

That's the way it is every day.

Sounds corny, doesn't it?

Even though it's something I don't make a point of broadcasting, I love it. No matter how busy my day is, I make it a point to stop by the apartment first thing after school, even if it's only long enough to stuff the warm, freshly baked cookies in my mouth and run out the door with that glass of milk.

Gran.

I love the stability she offers. Her love without condition.

Both amaze me. She's the mother of my step-mother. So only a barely connected relative. With no compelling reason to do so, she took me in when I was at my worst—"behaviorally challenged" was the nice term that my psychiatrist used in his report. And yet Gran had calmly withstood all my tantrums in the first six months there until I finally realized there was nothing I could do to make her hate me or reject me.

Looking back now at my first six months with her, I think I was testing her to see if she'd abandon me like my mother and my father had.

Sure, you can tell me a hundred times that my mother didn't die on purpose when I was born. You can tell me a hundred times that the decisions my father made were based on his greed. But the end result of both events meant that each of them, in different ways, abandoned me. Hurt me.

Gran hasn't.

That's what makes all of this so much worse. She's the one person in the world who has believed in me. And I'm going to end up doing to her what my father and mother did to me.

Hurt her badly.

This goes through my mind as I listen to Brianna and consider what she is telling me.

■ ■ ■

"Me spend time in jail?" I say to Brianna. "Are you nuts?"

Suddenly the hardness in her voice is gone. "I want to help you," she says softly. "Because I need *your* help."

I finally look at her fully. She tries a smile on me. I don't smile in return. Hurt fills her face. I feel bad and try to make up for it.

"You need my help," I repeat.

"Tyrone," she says, "Hale told me that you are running a drug business. That you've been picking up drugs every week at the Greyhound station in Des Moines and distributing them in Macon. . . ."

I flinch. How can Brianna know that? Hale and I had sworn we'd never tell anyone—and that included girlfriends—about our runs for Mitch. But now it was out in the open. And Brianna wasn't known for keeping her mouth shut, either.

I begin to think that maybe, just maybe, Brianna's right. Maybe Hale *is* setting me up for a fall.

So I nod. "Okay, I'll hear what else you have to say."

"I'm afraid," she says, "afraid that I'll get in big trouble. My folks have no idea I'm into drugs."

"Why you?" I ask. "What do you have to do with this?"

"Everybody knows Hale and I have been seen together a lot. So I'm probably going to get called down to the police station too. And Hale knows I use drugs," Brianna says. "I used to get them from him. But now I've been getting them from another source. And Hale's ticked off."

■   ■   ■

My veins feel like rainwater has just started to trickle through them. I get this icy sweat happening across

my back and chest. How many times had I gone
to the bus station with Hale? Too many.

I shivered. Worse, Hale had been the one who
always waited in the car while I walked up to the
counter to pick the packages up. So to anyone on
the outside, I *would* look like the lead dealer.

"This is where we help each other," Brianna says.
"Hale is gone now. I doubt he'll be around for court.
No, once he's in the hills, no one will be able to
find him."

"I didn't deal," I say, trying to defend myself.
"We were just delivering and—"

But it's not true, not really. Yet I don't even want
to admit this to myself. I may not have handed anybody pills like Hale did, but I knew what I was doing
when I picked up those boxes at the station and then
drove back with Hale to Macon to drop them off at
the bike shop. I'm not an idiot.

After the first run I'd been suspicious. After all,
who gives you a hundred bucks to just go pick up
vitamins? And why wouldn't you just have them
shipped directly to your door? By the second trip,
I'd known those packages had to be more than
vitamins. But the money was good, and I'd fooled
myself into thinking that all I was doing was picking
them up. It wasn't like I was dealing the drugs or
anything.

"I believe you," Brianna says, and looks so sin-
cere for a change that I almost believe her. "Hale
had us all fooled! I remember laughing and telling
him that I didn't need any vitamins or protein
supplements. I even teased him about being in the

vitamin business. But all along he was supplying drugs to the entire high school." She laughs ironically. "I mean, I even bought a couple pills myself. You know that because we tried them out together. If I'd known the stuff was coming from Hale, I could have saved some money."

I knew. And so did she. Getting drugs free or cheaper was the only reason she'd ever started going out with Hale Ramsey in the first place. Talk about betrayal. All the time he'd thought she was in love with him, she'd been using him. But so what? I too had betrayed Hale. Someone I called my friend. And now it must be *my* payback time.

"He's going to say it's me," I say slowly.

"No," she says, "not if he's back among the hillbillies."

"So what do you want from me?" I ask.

"Silence for silence. I'm guessing you kept your mouth shut at the police station. You're a lot of things, Ty Larson, but stupid is not one of them."

Silence for silence. I think I understand. But I listen and wait for her to say it.

"They're going to be asking a lot of questions about that party. Don't tell anyone about our night together. Or that I gave you roofies . . ."

I thought back to that night. The night I'd actually tried a roofie for the first time. I remembered the detached, floating feeling . . . and then waking up the next morning, not remembering anything that had happened.

"That's all," she said. "And in return, I won't tell what I know about your multilevel drug business."

I wasn't really a dealer. But would anyone else believe it after people at the Greyhound station confirmed I'd been in once a week to pick up packages? I thought about all the times that Hale had waited in his Camaro as he sent me inside. About the fact that *I* had been the one to sign for all the packages.

And I got angry. How could I have been so stupid?

Now Sammy was dead. I knew that pointing the blame at Hale wasn't going to change that. And I knew I'd played a role in Sammy's death too.

But Sammy had made a decision too. A bad decision. The kind of decision that wouldn't have killed most people. But it did kill Sammy.

Would getting Brianna, Hale, or me in trouble change anything?

No.

So I make another decision. "Yes," I say to Brianna. "It's a deal. Silence for silence."

Silence for silence.

Sammy died on a Saturday night. Five days later, not knowing that Detective Sanders was working behind the scenes to backtrack how Sammy died, I had participated in an after-school drug deal. It was just a few days ago, but I will always remember it.

Drug deal.

Yes.

Drug deal.

Those words sound so ugly. I can't deny it.

Hale and I had delivered merchandise to Miranda Sanchez.

Not merchandise. Drugs. There's no sense trying to sugarcoat what I did wrong. It's the world I want to fool, not myself.

Drug deal.

We had just walked into Mitch's bike shop, and it seemed like Mitch and Miranda were in a heavy-duty conversation.

Miranda didn't look her usual drop-dead gorgeous self. She looked like a woman who'd been awake for five days straight, and I wouldn't have been surprised if that were true. I doubt she'd slept much since Sammy died at the party at her house.

They broke up their conversation quickly, and Mitch sent her out into the parking lot to talk to Hale and me. Mitch called it "a formal introduction of sorts."

Hale seemed to know what was happening. I was a little more clueless.

After the formalities in the parking lot, with Hale leaning against my car as he puffed on a cigarette—well, not really formalities, since Miranda was in a mood that matched her appearance, and Hale was willing to be obnoxious on her behalf—I found out the reason for the discussion.

"So what're you looking for?" Hale asked Miranda.

"Huh?"

"You know, what do you need? What can you afford?"

"I guess I want a week's worth. Oh, well, why don't you just make it a month's worth?"

A sick feeling began to grow in my stomach. Picking up packages for Mitch was one thing, but selling the drugs was another.

When Hale and I were alone, I spoke very slowly and evenly so I'd stay in control. "Didn't know it had gone this far, Hale. Don't know that I like that."

degrees of guilt

"The dealing? Or the fact that I kept you out of the action?"

"Both," I said.

"Come on." His voice held irritation. "How much difference is there between picking the stuff up at the Greyhound station and actually making deliveries?"

"Lots."

"Ty, back home, there's no such thing as just a little bit shot. Either the bullet hits you or it misses you. You've been making pickups. You're part of it."

"Why didn't you tell me about the other end? The delivery end?"

"For the same reason we're having this conversation. You liked it, pretending to yourself that maybe there was a chance we really were picking up vitamins and health-food supplements. I didn't want to burst your bubble."

I thought about it. Thought about how I had wanted the money but none of the dirt that came along with taking it.

"I guess this makes us *dealers,* then, doesn't it?" I said, trying the word on for size. I didn't know if I liked the term, but Hale was right. Once I'd started picking up the packages, I was just as guilty as if I'd been delivering too. "You want to tell me exactly what it is we deliver?"

I emphasized the word *we.* After all, Hale had been my best friend for four years. If he was in this all the way, I would stand shoulder to shoulder with him.

"What do we deliver?" he asked and grinned.

tyrone's story

"Easy. All you have to know are colors. Orange. White. Blue." He grinned again. "White is the most popular. That's Brianna's favorite."

Guilt—more guilt—instantly stabbed me. She'd given me a white pill. That Hale had given her. That I'd taken. Suddenly I felt dirty. Very dirty.

Hale must have caught the look on my face because he playfully punched me on the shoulder. "Hey, lighten up. We're no different than the guys who delivered moonshine during the Prohibition. My family has a long and honorable history in that department."

"Yeah," I said. "Great."

And that night I was with Hale as he delivered the pills to Miranda. My first real drug deal.

None of this do I ever want the world to know.

So I've agreed to Brianna's deal.

Silence for silence.

As I walk up the steps to the three-bedroom apartment that is now my home, I wonder if Gran is going to be able to see the guilt and wretchedness all across my face.

■　■　■

Sure enough, just like the sun rises in the east, Gran is waiting back at the apartment. Sure enough, there are freshly baked cookies on a tray with a glass of milk. Sure enough, she is wearing an apron over the sweater and blue jeans that she wears in the apartment, versus the nice dresses she wears when she has to go out and be seen in public. She's old-fashioned like that—wants to put on her best appearance for others.

Her hair is white, cut short. I suppose someone seeing her for the first time would notice the heavy wrinkles that have settled on her face with age. But I stopped noticing those wrinkles a long time ago. What I do notice, every time, is her warm smile and the twinkle in her dark eyes.

Really. Twinkles. She is full of good humor, and along with the laughter that bubbles out of her, the twinkles are an outlet for her approach to the world.

Now, however, as she hands me the cookies and milk, her face and voice are grave. "Talk to me, Ty," she says. She points at an armchair opposite the coffee table in the middle of the room. "Things haven't been going well since your friend Sammy died, have they?"

Now that's an understatement. I nod. And take the armchair.

She sits on the couch and leans forward. "Well?"

"Nothing I feel like talking about, Gran."

I know she'll respect my wishes. She won't pry. But she surprises me with a different kind of question.

"Think about Moses in the Bible," she says. "And King David. And Saul who became Paul. Tell me what all three had in common."

I do think about it. I know my Bible history because of how I grew up. Bible and prayers at the table at every meal. Never aware, of course, that after the Bible devotions and prayers, my father would leave the table and dedicate his life to stealing funds without getting caught.

I tell myself I'm different than my father. I'm doing something just as wrong, but at least I'm not pretending to be a Christian as I do it.

"Moses," I say, keeping those other thoughts to myself, "led his people out of Egypt. King David helped establish the tribes in the land that God gave the people. Saul hated followers of Jesus, then converted to their faith and called himself Paul. I give up. What do they have in common?"

She smiles. "Each of them was a murderer. Moses struck someone dead in a fit of rage and hid the body. King David was having an affair, so he sent the woman's husband to the battlefront and arranged for the other soldiers to retreat so that man's death would be certain. Saul? Dedicated his life to killing Christians. Yet all are remembered as great men. They asked God for forgiveness. And got it. Even though they'd each committed one of the greatest sins possible."

"Gran, I—"

"Not finished, Ty. I want you to understand what it was like when Jesus appeared and started to tell people about God, his Father. Back then people believed they could not approach God unless they had first made themselves right enough to be in his presence. That's why they made sacrifices, punished themselves. All in atonement for how far short they were of God's perfection. They didn't dare approach him. Jesus, however, gave his listeners great hope. He told them that system of sacrifice was about to change. Because of Jesus, all you have to do is approach God, and he will make you right. Total reversal, Ty. Today Jesus doesn't stand in front of us like when he was walking this earth, but he still gives us that same message. You don't have to make yourself right to approach God, but approach him, and he will make you right."

"Gran, I–"

"Not finished, Ty. I want you to read this. Luke 15. Start at verse 11 and go to the end of the chapter."

She hands me the Bible that's always on the coffee table.

I read. Actually, I just skim. I'm familiar with it. It's the parable of the lost son. About a guy who goes to his father and asks for his inheritance, then runs away and spends it foolishly. When he's in the depths of poverty, he realizes he would be better off at home as a servant. So he goes home and begs his father for forgiveness.

"Done," I say, setting the Bible back on the coffee table.

"Not yet." There is firmness in her voice that I'm unaccustomed to hearing. "Read verse 20. Aloud. To me. It describes the son's journey back to his father. After the son hit rock-bottom and wanted forgiveness."

Reluctantly I pick up the Bible and do as she asked. My voice sounds strange to me. "'So he returned home to his father. And while he was still a long distance away, his father saw him coming. Filled with love and compassion, he ran to his son, embraced him, and kissed him.'"

I set the Bible down.

"Ty, make a picture in your head," Gran says. "How could the father have seen the son from a long distance away unless the father was scanning the horizon for him? Think about it. His son has rejected him, yet every day the father is searching the horizon, hoping for the son's return. And when the son finally turns and approaches his father, the father doesn't condemn him, but runs to meet him and hugs him tightly. That's love."

I do make a picture in my head. It gives me shivers.

"That," Gran says, "is how Jesus wants us to understand God the Father. If we always refuse to come home, God can't embrace us. But no matter what we've done wrong, all we need to do is reach toward God, turn back to him, and he'll reach back. He's always waiting, hoping for us to reach for him. And when we approach him, he'll forgive us."

I'm quiet, thinking about what she has said.

"You're troubled, Ty," she says. "It's very obvious to me. You don't have to tell me why unless you want to. I'm just saying that you are loved. By me. By God. By Jesus. When he came into the world to deliver the message, he meant it. Enough that when Jesus could have walked away from the cross, he chose instead to die, proving how much he meant what he said."

Gran stands. "I want to leave you alone to think about all this. That's what I'm asking. Just spend some quiet time and think about it."

She gets to the kitchen and half turns. "Remember, Ty. It doesn't matter where you're coming from. It matters where you choose to go."

Then I'm alone. With the Bible open in front of me. I know I am in a bad place—a real bad place. All because of decisions I've made and can't change.

I wish I would have known then what I know now.

(then)

"When sorrows come they come not single spies,
but in battalions."

Hamlet, Act IV, Scene 5

"Let me tell you something about her,"
Sammy said one night at the doughnut shop, when
we had our physics textbooks spread out on the
table in front of us. We'd been meeting once or
twice a week, ever since Mitch set me up at the bike
shop to help Sammy. "What makes it so frustrating
is that she's good friends with my sister. So it's like
she's within reach, but untouchable."

Sammy didn't have to tell me who the girl was.
Miranda Sanchez, of course.

It was ironic. I was totally, totally smitten with
Sammy's sister. Because Sammy and I were getting
to be better friends all the time, my situation was
no different than his. Kyra, as Sammy's sister, was
within reach, but untouchable.

Unlike Sammy, however, I kept that frustration

bottled inside me. I didn't want to say a word about it because of how disastrous my time with her had been.

"I can't figure her out," Sammy said, unaware of my yearnings. "New Year's Day she shows up, looking for Kyra, who was mad about the night before because—"

Sammy stopped. "Sorry. You were her date New Year's Eve, weren't you?"

I coughed theatrically.

"You should be proud of yourself, Ty. It's tough to make her upset. She likes to pretend she lives in a perfect world. What exactly did you do that night?"

"Can't tell," I said. "CIA secret. If you find out, your life may be in danger."

"Yeah, yeah," Sammy said. Traces of chocolate milk formed a dark mustache above his mouth. I wasn't going to tell him. More fun for him to find out for himself when he went home and looked in the mirror.

"Miranda . . . ," I prompted. "New Year's Day."

"She came over. Kyra was sleeping in. I cleared snow off the driveway so we could shoot hoops. I mean, isn't that a great girl? Looks like a beauty queen and is not only willing to play basketball, but plays a mean game?"

I nodded. Sammy would have found a way to say something just as enthusiastic about Miranda if she hated basketball.

"We're shooting hoops," Sammy continued, "and the noise wakes Kyra. She comes out, and just like that, Miranda leaves. I had to pretend that was cool, but still. I was just a time filler. Or so I think."

Sammy stared blankly at the open pages of the physics book. "The next day, the very next day, she calls for Kyra, telling me she wants to do something totally crazy. She says her New Year's resolution is to be a fun party girl, so I offer to help. Miranda goes out with me instead of Kyra."

I smiled. "No offense, Sammy, but I don't think you're going to appear in the yearbook as the school's party boy."

He gave me a wry smile. "I tried. At least that night. Miranda offered me a beer."

I gasped in fake shock, loud enough to draw looks from other tables.

"No, Sammy, no! A beer. An entire 12-ounce can of beer! Did you pass out?"

"Ha-ha," he said. "And no, I didn't pass out. I helped her make a snowman on Coach Reynolds' front yard."

I laughed. "That was you guys?"

A photo of the snowman had appeared in the paper that week. What made it interesting was the fact that a vertical line of three empty beer cans had been inserted into the fat, round middle section of the snowman's belly as buttons. The caption of the photo is what had made it so funny: Snowman's Beer Belly. Coach Reynolds hadn't found it funny. Rumor had it he wanted the beer cans dusted for fingerprints.

"That was us," Sammy admitted. "See, one beer and I become a totally irresponsible citizen."

"Let's forget about this physics stuff tonight and see what happens if I can get a half-dozen beers inside you."

Sammy made a face. "The stuff tastes like dirty bathwater. Ever noticed?"

"Ah," I said. "You get used to it. Besides, we all drink because the beer ads on television compromise our judgment. And, now that I think of it, Miranda looks good enough to be on one of those ads."

"That's the problem," Sammy replied. "We had all that fun. I was thinking that maybe she does like me more than a friend. Then, sure enough, she throws her arm around me and kisses me. Not just a peck on the cheek, either."

I had a flash vision of Kyra doing that to me. I nearly swooned. But I managed to stay casual. "And . . . ?" I prompted.

"As soon as she let go, it was like someone had dumped cold water over her. I could see it in her eyes. She pushed away like I was a freak. So the next day I had to call her and tell her that I didn't think it was a big deal and that we were still just friends."

"Ouch," I said. "The killer phrase." I spoke in a high, girlish voice. "I really, really like you, Ty. Let's just be friends."

Sammy nodded, miserable. "Every day I have to see her in school and remember that's all we'll be. Friends. It's a horrible thing, but you probably don't know anything about it."

"True," I said, hiding my reaction.

But I thought grimly, *Of course I know about it.*

Except it's with your sister. Except I don't even have a chance of being her friend.

Out loud I said, "You're right. I don't have a crush on Miranda, so I wouldn't know a thing about it."

"Ha-ha. Once again, too funny." Sammy scratched his left arm with his right hand. "You think maybe I should try to party more, like Miranda and Kyra. You know, join the crowd?"

"So that's it," I said. "You really don't need help with physics. You want to join me and Hale as renegades."

"I said party more, not become a total idiot."

It was my turn. "Ha-ha."

He sighed.

I hid my own sigh.

"Sammy, ever hear of a black hole in the universe? It forms after a super-sized star burns out and collapses on itself. Something a thousand times the size of the sun becomes a little ball about 10 miles across. One teaspoon of it weighs about as much as the earth itself. The gravitational forces are so strong that not even light can escape."

"Get out," he said.

"Sure. If you shone a flashlight beam nearby the dark hole, it would suck the light in and the light would disappear. Of course, you wouldn't really be able to do that, because if you were holding a flashlight close enough, you'd get sucked in as well, with every molecule of your body pulled apart and impacted into the black hole."

"Cool."

"Well," I told him, "that's love. It's like we have

tyrone's story

a decision in life. Stay far enough away that it doesn't hurt you. Or get close enough to wonder what it's about. But if you do get close enough, love draws every part of you inside and you're never the same."

"Amen." Sammy sighed again. "Amen to that, my friend."

A little over two weeks later, on a
Thursday, January 26, I walked onto the parking lot
of Fred's Discount Autos with 15 hundred-dollar
bills in my back pocket.

Facing the street, the front row of cars had a
used Lexus, a couple of shiny newer SUVs, and
even a Corvette. I didn't even get my hopes up.

I walked past the second row. Those vehicles
weren't quite as nice as the row facing the street,
but still good. But too good for me.

I walked past the third row.

The fourth row.

The last row was my destination. Those were the
vehicles I could afford.

A mean north wind plucked at the collar of my
coat. I hardly noticed. Part of me was excited about

purchasing my first car. And part of me felt lousy about it.

Fred Myers himself walked out of the mobile home that served as the office. His son had played on the Macon High Tigers football team, and because of it, I felt I could trust Fred.

He was a big man and wore a long coat. Slapping his arms against his sides against the cold, he recognized me immediately.

"Tyrone Larson," he said, sticking out a hand for me to shake. "Kicking tires again?"

There had been other times I'd walked through the lot, dreaming.

"Not in this weather," I answered. "This is the real deal. Finally going to buy something."

He grinned, showing me large white teeth. "Got a Corvette for you, in case you didn't notice."

"Take 1,500 bucks for it, and we've got a deal."

"Sure," he said.

"Really?"

"Yup. Fifteen hundred bucks is a great down payment."

"Ha-ha," I said.

He grinned again. "Fifteen hundred dollars, huh? Let me tell you something. I've got a car for you that's not a looker. And it's not the fastest. But for you, I'll do something I rarely do. I'll give you a six-month warranty. Anything major goes wrong, you can return it."

"Sounds good."

"It is." Fred was firm and serious. "I'm only making that offer because I know it's in great shape mechanically. That's the kind of car you should get at your age. Not flashy, but dependable."

I found myself nodding along with him.

"Not only that," he added, "but I'm not going to play the usual salesmanship games with you. It's listed at $2,500. You can drive it away, with a full tank of gas, for a thousand less than that."

"Um," I said skeptically, "it sounds too good to be true."

"Smart man," he said, smiling. "Anything that sounds too good to be true usually is. But I'm going to let you in on a secret. And I hope you remember it all your life."

I waited.

He was serious again. "Car lots like mine all across the country, we're not interested in selling cars." He must have caught the puzzled look on my face. "I know, I know. I've got cars lined up and filling my entire parking lot. So it looks like I'm selling cars. But what I'm really selling is financing."

I was still puzzled. But curious.

"Ty, you know about the television ads that promise no one will get turned away. Bad credit, no problem. Bankruptcy in your past, no problem. Those kinds of ads."

"Sure," I replied.

"Bad-credit customers like that, they pay maximum interest rates. I'm talking *maximum*. Rates so high that it's worth the lenders' risking money to them. The cars are just an excuse to get those kinds of people hooked to those high-interest loans. Over

tyrone's story

five years, for example, the interest paid almost matches the amount loaned out in the first place."

I was beginning to understand. "You sell financing."

"Exactly. Most of my customers come in with 50 bucks down and desperate for any kind of loan. That lets me charge them way more than what the car's worth. And I pass them on to a central lender where they get set up with a loan that's nearly as bad as extortion, and I get a piece of that, too. Someone like you, with an all-cash payment, is very rare. I can afford to sell you a car at a good discount."

Fred walked me toward the end of the last row. "What I'm saying," he continued, "is that most of my customers started making bad decisions when they were your age. Those decisions put them in positions later on where they were at the mercy of car dealerships like mine. I want you to always remember that, so you'll never be forced into a bad loan for a bad car. Got it? Look ahead and make good decisions that will take you where you want to go."

"Got it," I said. How I should have remembered that advice.

"Good." He stopped and pointed. "So here's your reward for saving up all that hard-earned cash."

Cash that I felt guilt over. All I'd done for some of it was make a bunch of trips to Des Moines with Hale. To pick up packages of "vitamins and health-food supplements." At least that's what Mitch called them. But then, Mitch warned us again and again not to get caught by the cops. Or, if we got stopped, to hide the packages. By the time I was ready to buy my car, I had already made an extra 300 dollars, just in three weeks. Easy money to add to my car fund. That, with the money I'd already saved since I was a little kid, and the savings account my parents had started for me even before I was born, gave me the total that was in my pocket.

I should have let that guilt tell me something. That I was already making bad decisions that would cost me later.

But I wanted a car too badly.

"What do you think?" Fred Myers asked. He was pointing at a green Escort.

A snot-green Escort.

What I was thinking was that it had better be a very mechanically sound car to make up for its ugliness.

"I'm telling you," he said convincingly, "for a first car, this is the best you're going to find in Macon. Fourteen hundred dollars."

I wondered if I kept my mouth shut if he'd drop it to thirteen hundred.

"Drive it for a day," he urged me. "Take it to an auto shop and have them check it out for you. I promise you'll find no problems."

Fred looked around. "Here's the truth. It belonged to my wife. And, honestly, I hated seeing it on my driveway. It's one ugly car. Great mechanical shape, but ugly."

"Yes sir," I said. "It certainly is."

But he was right.

It drove great.

But as I drove down the street, I wondered if I could ever drive far enough to get away from the nagging guilt that came with the car.

As You Like It.

A play written by William Shakespeare.

When Mitchell Wade announced in class that it was going to be the theatrical presentation for the spring of our senior year, the only thing I liked about *As You Like It* was the fact that it was going to give me a chance to enjoy Kyra's great acting. Other than that, I will complain bitterly to anyone who might listen about why William Shakespeare seems to represent high school English.

My theory is this. He's dead. He's not around to disagree with high school teachers and university professors about what his plays symbolize. That means they can come up with whatever interpretation they want and then inflict that interpretation on students.

Furthermore, he's been dead so long that none of his ancestors can disagree either. Nor are there ancestors in a position to make legal or monetary or copyright claims on the intellectual estate that William Shakespeare left behind in this world when he "shuffled off this mortal coil."

Now, that's a line from one of his plays. A pretty cool line. And that's why I'd never say anything bad about his writing. Just the opposite. He wrote some real zingers that I'll admire as much as any scholar. Ones I've jotted down in my notebook from time to time.

"Slings and arrows of misfortune"—another great line.

And these lines, from *As You Like It*:

> *"All the world's a stage,*
> *And all the men and women merely*
>   *players.*
> *They have their exits and their entrances,*
> *And one man in his time plays many*
>   *parts,*
> *His acts being seven ages. . . .*
> *Last scene of all, that ends this strange*
>   *eventful history,*
> *Is second childishness and mere oblivion;*
> *Sans teeth, sans eyes, sans taste, sans*
>   *everything."*

Once you know that *sans* means "without," it's good stuff. Profound stuff. About how each of us comes into this world, goes through childhood, becomes an adult, grows old, and dies. Cradle to the grave. Written in a way that is still fresh after all these centuries.

But is Shakespeare the only writer to have existed?

I know, I know. There are other authors, and teachers inflict their opinions of those writers on us as well. But I'd be willing to bet if you went to every high school in North America, there would only be one writer that students at every high school studied in common.

William.

Teachers will argue that it's valuable for our cultural understanding to know Shakespeare. Well, I'd argue right back that's only because they've chosen to force every new generation of high school students to learn about him, and because of it, his writing has become a cultural foundation. So what came first, the chicken or the egg?

Not that I blame teachers. It would take too much work to become the first teacher to study a different author. You'd have to write your own lesson plans and your own study materials instead of just dipping into the great ocean of material about Shakespeare lying around. And if you actually did all that work, you'd probably get angry phone calls from brainwashed parents who believe that if a kid doesn't learn about Shakespeare, he's not learning English. And angry phone calls from other parents who figure that if they had to suffer through Shakespeare a generation earlier, then so should the next generation.

tyrone's story

All of this is to say something very simple.

When Mitch Wade picked *As You Like It*, and when most of the students were fighting for the privilege of getting a role in the play, it was a matter of principle for me that I would never, ever let myself join the dogfight.

But that didn't mean I couldn't enjoy the spectacle.

■   ■   ■

The tryouts, of course, came well before the play itself. They took place in the gym on a Friday after-noon, the last Friday in January.

The Tigers would be playing basketball that night in the same place, but I doubt anybody there in the afternoon was thinking about it. Me included. I liked basketball about as much as I liked tryouts for a William Shakespeare play.

However . . .

Kyra was trying out for the play.

Kyra was a cheerleader and would be at the basketball game.

Brianna was trying out for the play.

Brianna was a cheerleader and would be at the basketball game.

So, like moths to a lightbulb at night, Hale and I were at the tryouts, in the back in the bleach-ers. Just like we'd be at the basketball game hours later.

I wasn't really paying attention to the first parts of the tryouts for the play. Sound echoed too much

in the gym, and if it wasn't Kyra, I wasn't interested. I was thinking more about moths drawn to
lightbulbs.

And wouldn't you know it? Only *male* moths
are idiotic enough to flutter and bump and attack
lightbulbs until they are so exhausted they fall to
the ground. And, wouldn't you know it, they do it
because of females.

Really.

It was in one of my science magazines. Male
moths depend on moonlight to help them navigate
in a straight line, keeping the moon's rays at a con-
stant angle as they fly in search of a female waiting
on a leaf. Moths will mistake a lightbulb on at night
in your back porch for the moon. When they fly too
close, they can't get their bearings. It causes them to
fly in tiny, tight circles until they are too disoriented
and confused to do much else.

Kind of like me around Kyra and Hale around
Brianna. Except we were dumber than moths,
because we knew we were disoriented and confused
and enjoyed it anyway.

I elbowed Hale as Brianna took up a script and
began to read. "Here's your girl," I said.

"I wish," Hale answered.

"So do something about it," I said. "Ask her out.
Tonight. After the game."

He grunted.

"I had the courage to ask Kyra out," I said.

"And how did that date go?" he asked. "It's been
nearly a month and you still haven't told me
about it."

"Just ask Brianna out," I said. "What's the worst that could happen? She says no."

How wrong that statement would be, but at the time, of course, I didn't know what I would know about her later.

"Tell you what," Hale drawled. "You ask Kyra out again, and I'll ask Brianna."

"Well . . ."

"You still carry a torch for Kyra. What's the worst that could happen? She says no. And if she says yes, maybe you'll do better with your second chance than your first."

"What makes you think the first was that bad?"

Hale snorted. "The fact you haven't said a word about it."

My silence was confirmation.

"So," he said. "Deal? You ask her and I ask Brianna."

"Let me think about it."

He laughed. "I know that means you'll do it. I just hope each of them agrees."

Hale didn't take his eyes off Brianna as she auditioned. She stumbled through the lines, laughing at her mistakes, and in short, did a horrible job. I wasn't going to point that out to Hale, though. I mean, you don't try to hit a fly on a tiger's head.

Then, finally, came Kyra. She had a shine to her eyes that I could spot even from my place back in the bleachers. And she nailed her lines. Without her script.

"'It is not the fashion to see the lady the epilogue; but it is more unhandsome than to see the lord the prologue. . . .'"

A lady as an epilogue? It made no sense to me. Plus I doubted there really was a word like *unhandsome*. But it didn't matter. She had me spellbound. And everyone else there. She spoke as if she were actually the character Rosalind.

"'. . . I charge you, O women, for the love you bear to men, to like as much of this play as please you: and I charge you, O men, for the love you bear to women—as I perceive by your simpering, none of you hates them, that between you and the woman the play may please. . . .'"

Love. Everything always came back to that. Love. I ached to watch her.

When she stopped speaking, the silence in the gym was as loud as any applause. Then the applause hit, a delayed reaction, like the suspenseful pause between a lightning bolt and the thunder that follows. Some even gave her a standing ovation.

I didn't clap, though. Neither did Hale. Guys who sit in the back of the bleachers and pretend not to care are definitely guys who never applaud.

I caught Kyra glancing our way. I wanted to smile, but she looked away again. And time began again.

One after the other, people read their lines.

Then Sammy lifted Miranda by the waist, setting her in the center of attention. Few others knew what I did—how much Sammy wanted this to be real life and not a play.

"Act four, scene three," Mitch called out.

They became Oliver and Celia. The names of the characters meant nothing to me. Nothing. But Sammy and Miranda, well, they shot the lines back and forth like pros . . . or real-life lovers. For once I really started to care about Oliver and Celia. Was disappointed when they finished.

Again there was applause.

Each looked at the other. I thought of what Sammy had told me, how Miranda had spontaneously kissed him that one time after building a snowman with him. It seemed like it might happen again.

The moment passed.

Yeah, I thought, he really does have it for her, and he's too stubborn to let her know it. And maybe she has it for him but won't admit it.

But they never had a chance to find out. Less than two months later, Sammy James was dead.

The same night as the tryouts I got the second chance I'd been waiting a whole month for—a second date with Kyra James.

You might wonder, why would I want to? Especially after the first date where she'd left me standing at the Holiday Inn, with tickets in my pocket and the first flakes of a snowstorm hitting me in the face?

After I'd vowed never to even speak to her again? After weeks of doing my best not to even look at her in class because of how it made my heart ache?

Sure, I was strong. Able to resist. Until the first opportunity where it looked like I might have a chance to go out with her again.

Our date took place after the basketball game that evening.

In spite of Sammy's efforts, the Tigers were getting killed. But that's not what mattered to me.

On the floor in front of the bleachers, for a moment, Kyra looked vulnerable and lonely. Just the type of woman who needed a white knight on a white steed. Okay, well, a science brain with an old, snot-green Ford Escort. I was probably the only person in the universe who liked it, but that's because it was my first car. I loved the feeling of freedom it gave me. But even as proud as I was of owning my own car, I did have too much awareness that other people might not be as fond of it.

I'll admit I might have looked a touch eager as I hurried down to her. But she looked so good in her purple cheerleader outfit that I just had to try again.

"So," I said to her above the noise of the gym, trying to act cool but feeling like I very much wasn't. "Need a ride? Want to go to the Den after the game?"

I really don't like the Tiger Den. All the people in there remind me of what I'm not. But I know Kyra likes to hang out there. And I figured my chances of her saying yes to that are better than yes to any other suggestion I might have. Not only that, but it would give me the chance to let Kyra know I finally had my own wheels, especially after forcing her to walk to the party on New Year's Eve that we didn't even attend.

"Megan's giving me a lift home," she answered quickly. Like it wasn't a big deal that I finally had my own wheels.

Without saying anything else—what else was

there to say?—I climbed back to my seat. I felt like everyone in the gym had just witnessed Kyra James turning Tyrone Larson down. Even so, that was all right. After talking with Hale during the audition for the play, I'd decided ahead of time the chance of her going out with me was worth the likelihood she'd decline.

Which meant I would be alone tonight after the game. Well, not quite alone. I'd be cuddled up with a *Scientific American* magazine. But, somehow, learning about ultrashort-pulse lasers didn't quite rate the same as spending time with Kyra.

Up in the bleachers, Hale must have seen the whole thing. "No sweat, buddy," he said, narrowing his eyes. "It ain't over till it's over."

Then he shoved the couple in front of us and jumped the last three rows of bleacher seats, landing a few feet from Kyra and Megan. I wanted to yank him away from Kyra. The last thing I needed was a hillbilly arguing my case for me. But instead of talking to Kyra, Hale went straight to Megan. It was a side of Hale I'd rarely seen—smiling, almost shy looking.

Minutes later he climbed back and sat next to me. "Done. You ask Kyra again if she needs a ride, and I'll guarantee she does."

"What are you talking about, Hale? You want me to strike out again?"

"You won't. I took care of that. Me and Miss I-should-lose-a-few-pounds Megan are hooking up after the game, leaving your poor little Kyra out in the cold."

"You and Megan?" Megan definitely wasn't the kind of girl Hale asked out. She was too . . . nice. And too chubby. "But what about Brianna? I mean, I appreciate this, man, but you were all set to ask Brianna out."

"Not to worry," Hale said, so confident I found myself believing him. "It's all taken care of."

■   ■   ■

Hale's quick thinking meant two things. One, Hale wouldn't be looking to hop in my Escort. And two, Kyra had just lost her own ride with Megan.

Even so, I told myself that I wouldn't ask Kyra again. Not twice on the same night, at the same basketball game. I had more pride than that.

However, I did arrange it so that I happened to be standing nearby right before halftime. So close, in fact, that she turned and looked startled to see me.

Then she smiled.

"Hey," I said, then gave myself a mental shot across the head with a two-by-four. Couldn't I come up with anything more sparkling than that? I mean, I was a guy who could not only say "Deoxyribonucleic acid," but understood how two polynucleotide chains arranged themselves in a double helix, with adenine always bonding with thymine and guanine with cytosine.

"Why are you back here?" she asked.

I was about to lie and tell her that I needed to go to the bathroom. But I couldn't lie, not to Kyra of all people. How much of a relationship would it be if it were based on dishonesty?

Naturally I sounded like an idiot when I did answer. "Change your mind?" I asked.

"If you're going to the Den," she said, "I could use a ride after all."

I looked down at my plain T-shirt. I wasn't even wearing anything with a Macon High Tiger on it. I'd never screamed at a pep rally. Or really spent much time at the Den.

"Okay." I'd go into a dungeon if that meant spending time with Kyra. *Thank you, Hale Ramsey!*

I couldn't think of anything else to say. And the halftime was about to begin. I knew she had some cheers to do.

"Later," I said.

I hurried back to the bleachers.

From up there I saw Kyra run out onto the court to lead the charge for one last cheer.

They did the human pyramid, with her on top, as always. Half of me wanted to tell the world that Kyra James had just agreed to go out with me after the game.

And half of me realized that she would never feel the same about me as I did about her.

But that wasn't going to stop me from doing my best to impress her.

The Tigers lost. Lost so badly, in fact, that Sammy and his jock pals just slunk off the court, dragging their feet, and disappeared into the school's locker room without a sound.

Ho-hum. Who cared. They all took this winning-and-losing thing too seriously anyway.

I had showed up at the game for one reason only—to watch Kyra cheer. Honestly, I love to stare at her. I just can't help myself. But sometimes watching her makes me blush. Me, a high school senior, believe it or not. You'd think I've never gone out on a date in my life. But there was something about Kyra James that made me a little uncomfortable, especially when she was in her cheerleading outfit. I worried that somehow she'd sense how uncomfortable I was and feel uncomfortable herself. So I had her coat ready to help her cover up.

"Let me get my coat–," she began to say and then stopped when I handed it to her. Immediately I felt stupid for looking so eager to help.

We joined the crowd that moved quickly toward the doors. Once we were outside, I caught a glimpse of the stars and drew in my breath. They were as beautiful as the night Kyra and I went on our first date. Or, should I say, the night we *started* to go on our first date. I hoped by now that Kyra would have forgotten my stupid comment about gravity and the difference between nuclear fission and nuclear fusion. It had blown any notion of romance sky-high.

We dashed for my Escort, and I was grateful that the darkness disguised the snot-green color that was so horrible in daylight.

I opened the door for Kyra on the passenger side. By the time I slid in behind the steering wheel, she was shivering.

I put the key in. Crossed my fingers that the Escort would start first try. Now, of all times, I didn't want to flood it like I had already done on two other occasions.

"Would you please turn the heater on?" she begged, her teeth chattering.

Couldn't I do anything right? I wanted to explain to her why I'd been so inconsiderate.

"I was thinking . . . ," I began, then realized how it would sound if I told her that I'd been worried about the car starting. It would make me look even worse than a jerk who made a girl sit in the cold without the heater on. I stopped myself and turned the key.

I breathed a sigh of silent relief when it started.

That hurdle jumped, I began to think about the Den. And all the cool people who would be there.

"Let's blow off the Den," I suggested. "And maybe go somewhere private." But even as those words escaped, I gave myself another mental slap with my imaginary two-by-four. *Somewhere private*. Talk about stupid. What had *that* sounded like to her? Like I thought I was a movie star in a Ferrari? Or that I had some other motive in mind?

"I don't think so." Her voice sounded like she'd taken my question the wrong way.

I couldn't blame her. Maybe a good part of me did mean it "the wrong way."

"I've got a six-pack in the trunk," I threw in, desperate to be alone with this dream girl. I knew that Kyra went to more than her fair share of parties. Would the fact that I had beer impress her?

She shook her head.

I tried to sound as cool as a jock. "You haven't gone teetotaler on me, have you?"

Then I saw her face and gave myself a mental slap number three. Like I had any say in what she decided to do.

"Get real, Tyrone," she snapped.

I didn't blame her. I shrugged, trying to hide my embarrassment.

"Just take me to the Den or take me home. I'm really tired," she said.

I hit the gas. My carburetor had been giving me

trouble. It stuck at times, and this was one of them. I heard the grinding of gravel against my tires and then a screech as the Toyota ahead slammed on the brakes.

I nearly started to apologize, then realized that would make me look weak. So I shut my mouth.

And I should have kept it shut. But half a block later, I said my next stupid thing. "So is D.J. going to be ticked off when he hears we went out?"

I was looking to edge into funny stories about D.J. and Sammy, and how Sammy had stepped in during freshman year and ended the feud between Hale, me, and D.J. But Kyra took it wrong. And because of my track record, I couldn't blame her.

"You and I are *not* going out," she fired back in a voice edged with frost. "And D.J. doesn't own me."

I thought back to what Hale had told me—something about a party. "I thought you and D.J. were partying tomorrow night."

"So what?"

"Easy girl." I put my hands up, trying to look as cool as I wanted to sound. At least until the Escort hit a bump and I had to grab the steering wheel in a hurry. So much for looking cool.

It was silent in the car until we were several blocks from the Den. I pulled up to the curb. Hopefully the car was far enough away from the Den no one would see Kyra getting out of something that ugly. She deserved better.

It remained quiet as we walked in the cold. I wanted to turn around. This wasn't going to work. I couldn't say anything right. I was only making an idiot of myself. But what was I going to do? Just abandon her in the dark?

By the time we got there, the booths at the Den were already full. When we walked in, some juniors—jocks, naturally, since she was a cheerleader—waved at Kyra. She waved back. Somehow that simple wave only increased my loneliness . . . and the differences between us. But I wasn't ready to give up yet.

I saw that there were only two tables left, one near a booth. Kyra was peering toward the back of the Den, so I steered her with one hand on her shoulder toward the table. I didn't want to lose that table.

Dylan Gray, her next-door neighbor, waved at her. She waved back. He was the kind of guy who's as straight as you can get—the no-partying, churchgoing type. But he and Kyra still seemed to be great friends. Or were they more, and they just didn't know it? I wondered. Then, suddenly, it hit me—*That's the guy for her.* It seemed so right, my depression grew worse.

I kept my hand on Kyra's shoulder long enough to point her in the right direction.

Strange, badly as I knew this evening was going, I felt happy to have done one thing right. Taken control, found a table, guided her to it. I dropped my hand from her shoulder right away, though. I didn't want to give her the wrong impression—that I had my hand on her shoulder because I thought I owned her or that I wanted other people to think the same.

We sat at the table. I realized that the waitress

was too busy, so I quickly stood and asked Kyra what she wanted.

"Diet Coke?" she replied.

I nodded. I pretended the people in front of me were an army in the way of me getting Kyra a handful of diamonds. I elbowed my way through and called out her order. Plus a milk shake and sandwich for me. This didn't look like a promising evening, so I intended to enjoy *something* about it.

I couldn't think of anything to say when I returned with her Diet Coke. Not that I *really* couldn't think of anything. The opposite. My mind was whirling with thoughts. But I couldn't pick a single one to speak out loud.

Kyra smiled her beautiful smile. "What did you think of tryouts?"

"What do you think of Mitch?" I asked in return.

"He's okay," Kyra said. But her face was like a blank page, as if she wasn't paying any attention to what I was saying. Then I caught her looking over her shoulder at Dylan. That feeling hit me again. The one that told me she's right for him and he's right for her and me trying to put Kyra into my life is no different than taking a hawk off the wind currents and locking it in a cage.

"He's got something, doesn't he?" I said. "Dylan."

Kyra turned back to me. "He does," she admitted, as if it truly were occurring to her for the first time. "He's centered. He knows what he believes in. And he lives that way too."

We both knew she was talking about his Christian faith. But who wants to bring up religion on a Friday night date at the Den?

"Funny," I commented. "You go to church. My dad used to be part of a Christian organization. We should have it too."

She smiled. A truly genuine smile. "Maybe we do," she said. "We're just fighting it."

I realized she'd relaxed because we were having a conversation, for once, that wasn't based on any ulterior motives. Like trying to impress her. Or make her laugh. Or have her think I was cool. Or make her like me.

"Fighting it," I repeated, then shook my head. "Do you have any idea why my dad isn't around anymore?"

She nodded. "Diverted funds, or something like that. At least that's what I heard."

"Stole money. Plain and simple. He's in jail. Now you tell me why I should want any part of what he believed in. Of what he tried to convince the world to believe about his faith."

She thought about that for a second. "Remember on New Year's Eve, when you told me about the chemistry pranks?"

I nodded.

"Remember? You said you learned a lot of it from ninth-grade chemistry. You also told me the story about your first day in that class. Mr.—"

I grinned. "Mr. Bladesworth."

I'd been inspired to think that science was
cool because of one person.

Mr. Bladesworth.

I'd told Kyra about the day that Mr. Bladesworth
stood at the front of the lab, holding a beaker of
what looked like apple juice. He was short, with
a bald head and fringes of hair above his ears. It
looked like he'd been teaching since before the
invention of cell phones.

He introduced himself, then pointed at the flask.

"The first thing I want to teach you is that
chemists must never be afraid to use their senses
of smell and taste or touch when it poses no danger. For example . . . is this apple juice or apple-
cider vinegar?"

Holding the beaker up with his left hand, Mr. Bladesworth moved his right hand and dipped his index finger into its contents. He lifted it out again and put the finger in his mouth.

"What do you think?" he said.

"Ha-ha," one of the big kids at the front of the class said. "Nice try. There's no way you'd be tasting vinegar. It has to be apple juice."

Mr. Bladesworth walked over and handed the kid the beaker. "Test it yourself," Mr. Bladesworth said.

The kid stood, tilted the beaker, and gulped. Then choked and sputtered and gagged. He clutched his throat. "That's horrible!" he gasped.

"No," Mr. Bladesworth said, "that's cider vinegar." He smiled at the class. "And that's the second thing I wanted teach you. A chemist must always use his or her powers of observation."

"Sir . . ." It was the big kid again. "May I go to the bathroom? I think I'm going to be sick."

"Certainly."

The kid bolted.

"As I was saying," Mr. Bladesworth said, "you must rely on your powers of observation."

He held the beaker aloft, and once again dipped his right index finger into what was left of the contents of the beaker. He pulled his finger out.

"If you had watched closely enough," Mr. Bladesworth said, "you would have noticed I put a different finger in my mouth."

He demonstrated, and sure enough, he tasted a different finger.

■ ■ ■

"Mr. Bladesworth," I repeated to Kyra above the noise in the Den. "What about him?"

"Tyrone, ever notice the rest of us aren't major science . . . um . . . people?"

"You mean science freaks."

I was rewarded with another smile.

"Science people," she repeated. "Do you think that's because chemistry is boring, or because we didn't have the right teacher for it?"

I gave it some thought. "I think the right teacher could make it a lot more interesting."

"I agree," she said. "So it's not chemistry at fault, but the person representing it."

"I suppose."

"So is Dylan's faith wrong, or have the wrong people in your life represented it? I mean, I don't know much about your father, but . . ."

"Tell you what," I threw in. "How about closing that subject right now?" I stood. "Let's go. I don't feel like being here."

At my sudden anger her face lost its animation. "Fine," she said quietly. At the door she stopped. "I don't see Hale and Megan."

"Neither do I."

But I knew she hadn't stopped to look for them. She was using that as an excuse to stop and make sure that Dylan saw her leave with me. And because I was in a bad mood, it made me want her to feel the same bad mood.

"Wave good-bye to Dylan," I said. "That is, if he even looks up from his fun time with Taylor."

When Kyra stiffened, I knew the shot had hit home. And I felt instantly bad about it. Why did this love thing mix me up so much?

We'd just stepped outside, when who should come strolling up the sidewalk but Hale and Brianna. Brianna, as in not Megan.

"Howdy!" Hale waved, and Brianna grinned.

"Where's Megan?" Kyra asked.

Hale shrugged, then winked at me. That's when I knew he'd planned to dump Megan all along. *Megan didn't deserve that,* I thought. Somehow the thought of what Hale had done made me a little sick. It seemed so heartless.

Evidently Kyra understood what had happened too. "Let's get out of here," she said, sounding disgusted.

Halfway to my snot-green Escort, Kyra surprised me by asking for some of the beer in my trunk.

"Sure," I said. Earlier I'd thought it would be cool to sit somewhere and drink beer with her, just as I did with Hale on the weekends. But now it distinctly seemed like she was more interested in beer than me. That it was just convenient for her that I had it.

We drove to a spot behind the football field and split the six-pack. Kyra sure wasn't like her brother, Sammy, who never went to parties. I hadn't heard of the guy even drinking one beer, other than the time with Miranda when they had built the snowman. And yet here was his sister, downing three beers in one shot. It was hard to believe they were even from the same family.

After my second beer, I was still in a horrible mood. I hoped the third would help.

By Kyra's silence the whole time, I guessed she felt the same.

When we finished, I asked, "Got a cell phone?" Those words were the first we'd spoken the entire time the car was parked.

"Yeah."

"Better call a cab," I said. "I'll pay for it. I'm not driving."

"I'll walk."

Just like that. She got out and headed home.

I sat in the car. Staring out the windshield at the stars. The beautiful stars that shone light at me from an unfathomable distance. I tried to take comfort in thinking through the science behind that light.

But all that hit my mind were questions about God. Questions like . . .

Was God really there, somewhere in or beyond all the galaxies of stars? Or was he simply a product of someone's imagination? my imagination?

Did I somehow, in the back of my mind, believe in God enough still from my childhood that I'd defended him—or at least the scientific bases of my theory about him—in Mitchell Wade's class almost three weeks ago?

And, if God did exist, then why did he let my mother die even before I got to know her? before she got to know me?

And how did my dad, who had claimed to be
a Christian, go so wrong?

As the night got chillier, so did I. But no answers
came from the sky, and my mood didn't change.

And the beer?

It didn't help at all.

■   ■   ■

The next morning, I woke up with a headache. And
the bad mood still hadn't gone away.

Beer was not the answer.

But I wasn't smart enough to learn that lesson.

Because waiting down my road of life was a
night when I would drink too much beer again
and try out something even stronger. Then I would
regret my actions too.

Except that regret would be worse.

Much worse.

The drive to Des Moines from Macon

generally took about 45 minutes. Hale always took
Mitch's advice about breaking the speed limit. By
going exactly six miles an hour over, it was unlikely
we'd get a violation enough to be ticketed. Hale
hated not opening up the carbs on the Camaro, but
he knew the car was a magnet for cops.

We'd been making the trip once a week without
fail since Mitch had first given us the chance. And
the money.

By now we had it down to a routine. Hale would
pull up in the no-parking space. I'd run in with a
signed permission letter from Ethel Ethridge, sign
for the package delivered to her name, and run out.
From there, we'd grab a burger and turn around
back to Macon.

"Hey," I said, turning down Hale's CD player. "This ever bother you?"

"Are you kidding? Travis Tritt? You could play his music loud as you wanted and I wouldn't ever care."

"I mean what we're doing."

"Cruising down the highway with my best bud? Listening to Tritt? How could life get better?"

It was obvious to me that he was avoiding my real question.

"Come on, Hale. I'm talking about picking up these packages."

"Just packages," he said. "Not my business what's inside them."

The highway hum was comforting. His evasions were not.

"Hale," I pressed, "we get a hundred dollars each. Once a week. Mitch is giving us two hundred dollars a week to go to Des Moines."

"And?"

"And Greyhound does go to Macon. He could have the packages delivered there and save all that money he's paying us."

"No, no, no." I heard the grin in Hale's voice. "IRS, remember? That's why he's doing this."

"Sure," I answered. "He's spending two hundred a week to save on taxes. Actually more. See, it takes probably five hundred a week gross for him to net out two hundred after the taxes he does pay. Five hundred."

"Gross. Net. I'll have to take your word for it. Your old man's the bean counter."

Was the bean counter, I mentally corrected on Hale's behalf. Until he made a long-term visit to a federal hotel with bars. Iron bars. Not mini-bars.

Hale wasn't going to take my hints, so I decided to flat out say it. "Hale, what if the packages don't contain vitamins and health supplements?"

"Are you suggesting illegal substances?" Hale's drawl made his formal use of language verge on hilarious.

"I am," I said.

"Remember Prohibition?" he asked.

"No."

"Me neither. That's my point." He paused, waiting for me to tell him I understood. Since I didn't, I couldn't.

"Prohibition," he explained. "When all alcohol was illegal. Bootleggers made a fortune getting it to people. And the reason you don't remember Prohibition times is because now alcohol's legal."

"And?"

"Government says something is wrong one time, then changes its mind and says it's okay another."

"And?"

"I ain't saying what's inside these packages is anything but vitamins and health products. But *if*," he emphasized again, "*if* it turns out to be something that the government has banned at this point in time, I'm not prepared to carry a lot of guilt over it, because it's obvious to me that government laws are most often stupid and more often than not changed later."

"Oh."

"I'm getting paid for my time and so are you. It's as simple as that. Why don't you leave it that way?" Hale turned up the volume, and Travis Tritt filled the silence.

Seconds later Travis began a love ballad, and Hale sang along with it at the top of his lungs. I couldn't help but grin into the darkness, even with my unsettled feelings about what we were doing by going to Des Moines every week for Mitch.

When the song was over, it was Hale's turn to lower the volume. "Bri's only 17," Hale said.

I considered this to be totally out of the blue, but I didn't say so. Hale often had a way of edging backward into conversations.

"She doesn't turn 18 until March," he continued. "And you know what?"

"What?"

"I'm going to ask her to marry me on her eighteenth birthday."

"Does she know that?"

Since the Tiger Den date, Hale and Brianna had started going out. But I was pretty sure marriage was the last thing Brianna Devereaux had on her mind . . . well, at least marriage to Hale Ramsey.

"Surprise," Hale said. "But what a great one. I've already started looking for a ring. Six months from now she'll be Mrs. Hale Ramsey."

"Six months ago you were the guy who swore he'd never settle down. What was your saying? 'Too many women, too little time.' "

"That was before Bri. It's been over a month

since we first went out after that basketball game, and the feeling gets stronger every day. You'll find out what it's like when the love bug hits you, pal."

"Already know," I said. "Remember? Kyra?"

"How long you going to hold that torch?" he asked.

"Not holding it. It's holding me."

"Poor guy. Let me tell you, when a woman loves you back, there's nothing greater in the world."

"Hale?" I turned up the volume again and half shouted above it.

"Yeah?"

"Keep talking mushy like that and I'm going to puke."

Poor Hale.

One night later, on Friday, I was riding shotgun
in Hale's Camaro. I hadn't been there on a Friday
night since Hale and Brianna had started dating
because Hale usually reserved Friday nights for her.
He didn't apologize to me, his best friend, for this
change in protocol. I didn't expect that he should.
I understood. Like Hale told me repeatedly, Brianna
was a lot cuter than I was.

On this Friday, though, Brianna was out of town,
visiting a cousin.

Or so she'd told Hale.

We were in the Camaro, listening to *Tumbleweed
Connection*, a really old CD recorded by Elton John.
Hale liked country music. I didn't. This was one of
our compromise CDs, because it was a weird album.
Lots of twangy stuff.

We were on our twentieth lap down Main Street, and that, combined with the twangy music and Hale's humming, had put me into a stupor.

"Hey!" Hale turned down the music.

I blinked a few times. "What? Is it time to turn around again? So soon?"

"Funny, funny, Mr. Sarcasm." He reached across from behind the steering wheel and punched my left shoulder. "Look."

He pointed out the passenger window, his arm so close to my mouth I could have chomped it. Instead I followed the line of his arm, sighted down his finger like it was a rifle.

"Good spotting," I said. "That's called the Tiger Den. It's a place where—"

He punched me again. "The Porsche. That's Mitchell Wade's."

Now passing the Den, headed in the opposite direction we were going, was the Porsche.

"Amazing powers of deduction," I said. Around most people I kept my mouth shut. Around Hale I was able to speak my thoughts freely. "Let's see. This is Macon. The probability of a stray Porsche in this town at any given time is nil. Since Mitchell Wade is the only person in Macon who owns a Porsche, we can safely conclude—"

"Brianna was driving it," Hale said.

"What?" I straightened. "Brianna?"

Hale reached a stop sign. Cranked the steering wheel hard. Gunned the motor. The back end of the Camaro slid around. It was a slick U-turn. Something my new-to-me Escort could never accomplish. Which was why we cruised Main in the Camaro.

"Brianna," he repeated. "It looked like Mitch was on the other side. With his arm around her."

"But she's at her cousin's," I said. "Didn't you tell me that she was at—"

"Because that's what she told me. And now . . ."

Hale didn't finish. He started to close the gap between the Porsche and us. "They're headed out of town. I wonder where?"

His hillbilly accent had thickened considerably. Since moving here to Macon, there were times when he spoke and it was barely noticeable. But when he was angry or nervous or stressed out in any way, it came back like a boomerang.

"Slow down," I said.

"No. She's my girl. She's driving another man's Porsche. And he's done gone octopus on her."

I did a mental translation: *He's putting his arms everywhere.*

"Hale, there's probably a real good reason for this."

"Like what?"

"Whatever it is, you won't find out if you get close enough for her to know you're following."

Hale didn't answer. But he took his foot off the gas and eased back. By now we'd reached the edge of town. The streetlights on the sides of the road had ended. The Porsche, ahead of us and now in a higher speed zone, had pulled away again. We could only see it by its distinctive taillights and the beam of headlights in front of it.

"Man," I said, "are you sure it was her?"

"I know my girl."

Hale accelerated again, gently, and we stayed a half mile behind.

"This don't surprise me none," Hale said, his hillbilly accent strong. "Mitchell Wade looks at the girls in a certain way, and they all look back at him the same way."

His voice reflected such hurt, I was compelled to put Brianna's action into a good light. "For all you know, they might be going somewhere to buy you a birthday present."

"He had his arm on her shoulder, Ty. He was leaning into her."

I could think of nothing to say. After what Hale had told me only the night before about how much he loved her, any words would be monumentally insignificant compared to this apparent betrayal inflicted on him. And for it to be Mitchell Wade . . .

"I'll tell you what hurts," Hale continued. "Every day, going to Mitch's bike shop after school. Hanging out with him and the others. And here he does something like this. What are they going to do—pull over and park?"

So Hale *had* been thinking my thoughts.

"Love is a sword," I said. Visions of Kyra filled my mind. Beautiful, perfect, unattainable Kyra. "Pierces your heart."

"Not a sword." Hale grunted. "Velcro."

"Huh?"

"Come on, you ever looked at Velcro close?

Thousands and thousands of tiny plastic hooks. And when you try to pull it loose, each one of those tiny hooks holds on as tight as it can until it finally rips loose. That's love. Brianna and me. I got thousands of them little memories. And thinking of her with someone else rips each one of them memories from my heart."

Hale had turned down the music. Now the wind noise of highway speed was the backdrop.

"You're my best friend," he said. Plain and simple. He'd never said anything like it in the years since we'd met as freshmen hanging on coat hooks by our underwear. "Even so, I've never told you why I ended up in a juvenile detention center."

"You broke into a service station late one night. You told me about it once. Looking for tools and parts for the car you wanted to work on as soon as you turned 16. Had the wheelbarrow loaded when the police arrived."

"That's the reason I let everyone think. But tell me, isn't it kind of stupid to break into a place and throw things in a wheelbarrow while the alarm is ringing? 'Specially when the service station is less than a mile from the state troopers?"

Hale stared straight ahead, focused on the tail-lights of the Porsche that carried his girlfriend and the man with his arm around her shoulders.

"Can't tell you how many times people back home commented on that. 'Stupid hillbilly kid' is what I heard again and again and again. 'Dumber than a bag of hammers.' Let me ask you something honest. Did I ever strike you as stupid?"

"Nope." That was the truth. And an easy answer. Hale was definitely not stupid.

"Except for falling for Brianna, I'll agree with you. The reason I broke into that service station was because I *wanted* to go to the juvie center."

"Wanted?"

"Ty, back in the hills, Ramseys have been on the run from the law from the beginning. It's almost tradition. If I didn't want to get caught, I could be still hiding, going from one family to the next. Had I really wanted those tools and parts, I'd have hot-wired a pickup truck, backed through the front window of a service station on a quiet country road, loaded it, and been gone in five minutes. But I used a wheelbarrow, walked it through the front door, smashed the glass, set off the alarm, and took my time. As it was, I still began to wonder if the cops would ever get there."

"You *wanted* to get caught." I wasn't sure if I understood him right.

"I've told you funny stories about my family," Hale said. "The bad ones I've kept to myself. Daddy likes to drink, and when he does he gets mean. Real mean. And that's only the tip of the iceberg. Let's just say it came to a point where I realized that while prisons are designed to keep people in, it also works the opposite. Once you're in prison, people on the outside can't get at you."

This was definitely not the time for a smart-mouth comment. Hale must have been vulnerable because of what was happening with Brianna. The sadness was leaking out of him. Just listening was the best thing I could do as a friend.

"Had a cousin," Hale continued. "Maybe four years older than me. Got out of prison, met his girl and his best friend on a Saturday night, went to a bar together. The best friend gave my cousin's girl a compliment, but my cousin took it wrong. They started arguing. Bouncer told them to take it outside. They fought. My cousin kicked his friend in the head when he was on the ground. Walked away. Other people walked around him, lying on the pavement with blood coming out of his head. Three hours later a cop noticed him. Called an ambulance. Too late. Cousin's best friend was dead. Cousin went back to prison."

Hale sighed, just loud enough to be heard above the wind noise. We were going 65, only five miles an hour above the speed limit. Matching the pace of the Porsche, a half mile in front of us. We were the only two cars on the straight, flat stretch of highway. In daylight I knew we'd be seeing shriveled cornstalks in the fields, like unburied skeletons.

"Granddaddy shot a man dead in a moonshine dispute," Hale continued, "and spent 10 years in a federal prison. Two brothers grow weed in a nearby state forest, got the crop booby-trapped in case federal marshals look too close. The list goes on, Ty. Back in the hills where I come from, the law don't mean nothing. The Ramsey brood is like a big old spider's nest. Blood kin and in-law kin spread out for about 30 miles, and we have secrets that fester and fester from one generation to the next."

Both of Hale's hands were on the steering wheel, like he was gripping it hard. Usually Hale drove with one hand resting lightly on the wheel. Ahead the taillights of the Porsche were unblinking beacons.

"Back in those hills, there's an abandoned mining shaft," he said. "Top of it's hidden in bushes. If you don't know where it is, you could step into the bush and disappear. Most of the Ramsey men—all my uncles—and my cousins know exactly where it is. I've been there too. Stood there with my daddy—he was sober that day—and listened as he dropped big rocks down the shaft. Not once did I hear it land. Some think the shaft is two miles deep. That's the place . . ."

Hale paused. Stared ahead for a few seconds like he was picturing something. "That's the place, it's been said for a hundred years, where the Ramseys drop the bodies of those that cross them."

He half turned his head. "That give you a picture of my family?"

"Yeah," I said softly. Not knowing why he was telling me this.

"I wanted to get away from them. From juvie, I wrote my aunt up here. She'd wanted to escape too and found a way out. I hoped she might take me in. And until tonight, I never once missed my family. Not in four years."

Hale stared again at the taillights. "Following that car is breaking my heart, Ty. Makes me want to be back amongst the people I know I can't trust. See, back there I never expected much out of people. Here I actually believed Brianna was my girl and always would be. That's what makes it so disappointing. The only thing that would surprise me more is if you turned against me. If that ever happened, I'd be back in Hazard County so fast, just to be in a world that at least I understood. . . ."

Hale always talked—a lot. But I'd never heard him talk so much in one stretch since we'd met. Especially not about something so personal.

"Maybe Brianna is—"

"I appreciate what you're trying to do, Ty. Believe me, I've been trying to think of a good reason she would be out on a Friday night with that man. But—"

He stopped. Looked in the rearview mirror. "Shoot."

I turned and saw. Red and blue flashing lights. Approaching fast.

"What are the chances the trooper's going past us?" I asked.

A second later as the trooper pulled up behind us, the siren answered my question.

"Shoot!" Hale repeated. He began to pull over to the shoulder.

Ahead, the taillights of the Porsche slipped away. Taking Brianna and Mitchell Wade beyond Hale's reach.

I felt bad for Hale, but also bad in another way too. What if we'd had one of Mitch's packages with us when the cops stopped us?

After that night, I was never quite able to get rid of that fear. The "what if" question stuck with me on all my remaining runs to the Greyhound station in Des Moines. What if we got caught with these packages of "vitamins" that weren't vitamins? What then?

But even the fear wasn't enough for me to make the move to get out. The money was too good. Too easy. And nobody was getting hurt. At least not yet.

Twenty-four hours later, on a Saturday
night, I was alone.

I'd called Hale, but he'd declined another round
of Main Street cruising. Said he wanted time by
himself and was going to drive the highway to get
Brianna out of his system.

Sammy was busy too.

That about covered all the friends I had.

So I stayed at the apartment and tried to distract
myself with a book on the nature of time and light.
Great stuff, huh?

The doorbell rang.

I heard the chime from my bedroom, where, book
in my lap, I'd been staring at the aquarium screen
saver on my computer.

I thought maybe Hale had changed his mind.
Decided to pick me up instead of calling by phone.

Then Gran knocked on my door.

"A young lady here to see you," Gran whispered as she cracked open the door to my bedroom. I heard a giggle in her whisper. "A very beautiful blonde."

Until that very second I had been at the bottom of a dark chasm, sinking in black oozing slime as horrible reptiles slithered around me. Nobody loved me. Suddenly my spirits felt as if the sun had shone brightly, all the way to the bottom of the pit! As if bluebirds of happiness were flying around my head!

Kyra! Here to give me a second—no, a third—chance. I'd keep my mouth shut, be cool, not let her know that I adored every fiber of her entire being.

"Hang on," I said.

I stood and looked in the mirror. Hairs were standing up. I licked my palm, slicked down the hair. I grabbed my bottle of Hugo Boss cologne and gave a quick spray under each of my arms. I tested my breath by blowing in my palm and sniffing the air that bounced back. I decided I needed something. No toothpaste in here, and if I went to the bathroom first before seeing Kyra . . . well, the apartment was so small she'd see me from the living room when I left the bedroom. And that might look suspicious. So I squirted some cologne into my mouth.

I turned to the door. That's when I noticed I had an audience.

"Gran!" I said. She'd kept her head inside the door. Was grinning at the cologne spray to my mouth.

"Good for you," she whispered. "She's beautiful. This one looks like a keeper."

Gran pulled her head out.

Kyra! I was most definitely not going to tell her my thoughts about the bluebirds of happiness. Only a moron would do that. And I'd already been enough of a moron around her.

I managed to refrain from running down the hallway to the front entrance of the apartment.

Even so, when I saw the beautiful blonde waiting just inside the door, I stopped so quickly it was like walking into an invisible sheet of Plexiglas.

"Brianna, what a surprise."

■　　■　　■

"I hope it was a nice surprise," Brianna said. "I didn't want to be alone tonight. Not after my big argument with Hale today. And I really need help with my homework."

We were walking down the street, away from the apartment, toward her house, a couple of blocks away.

"It was a nice surprise," I said. Then I realized there had been no enthusiasm in my voice. "Yeah," I repeated, faking happiness on this attempt. "You and Hale . . ."

"Last night I went for a drive with Mitchell Wade," she said. "I called Hale today and told him about it. He went ballistic. All jealous and everything. Wouldn't even let me explain why. As we speak, he's on the interstate. Said he was going to drive and drive until I was out of his heart."

"You and Mitch went for a drive last night?"

"Sure. Not a big deal. But Hale doesn't see it that way."

"Just a drive?"

"Now you're sounding like Hale." She laughed. "Would you turn down the chance to drive a real Porsche?"

On a Friday night. With Mitch. Out into the country.

If I were Hale, I'd be mad too.

Brianna clutched my arm and drew herself up to me. "It's cold, don't you think?"

I was thinking about Hale cruising down the interstate while I walked here with Brianna. But Hale would know this wasn't a big deal. One, I wasn't some California guy that all the girls adored, able to take them out in a Porsche. Two, Hale knew I was crazy about Kyra. Three, this wasn't the first time I'd helped Brianna with her homework. Ever since she'd started dating Hale, she'd asked me plenty of times.

"Really, Tyrone, it's very nice of you to offer to help me with my chemistry homework tonight."

"Saturday night. What else is a guy going to do?" I kept my voice light, but in my mind, I had already answered my question. *Walk around with Kyra. Just like this. With Kyra hanging on to my arm.*

Brianna laughed. "You said that with just the right touch of sarcasm. Impressive."

And she pulled herself tighter to me.

■ ■ ■

Brianna lived in one of the nicer neighborhoods, maybe a block away from Kyra. When I thought about it, the two of them had a lot in common. Same neighborhood. Same age. Same activities at school.

And yes, same kind of looks.

Brianna, like Kyra, had the long hair and the nice clothes. But to me, and for me, Brianna had a hard look to her face, like she was a cheap imitation of the real thing. Brianna had an edge. It was one of the things Hale loved about her.

Maybe I was thinking about their sameness because I was missing Kyra so much. Or maybe because a part of me enjoyed, secretly, the way that Brianna held my arm as we walked and made me feel stronger.

■ ■ ■

Her parents weren't home.

We sat in her living room in front of a gas fireplace that was operated by a remote control.

Her chemistry homework was scattered across the coffee table in front of the couch, with the cozy fire burning on the other side. Because the lights were dimmed, the fire put a glow across Brianna's face.

"Let's have a beer," she suggested.

"Bring it on," I said, still feeling bruised by Kyra.

Brianna slipped away to the kitchen and returned with two cold cans of beer. She cracked mine open and handed it to me. Then cracked hers open and sat beside me on the couch.

Brianna giggled. "I like you, Tyrone," she said. "Always have."

She toasted me with her beer.

As the firelight moved across her face, a thought flashed through my mind, a thought I tried to push away. A thought I knew Hale would hate me for, and a thought I hated thinking.

But it was there anyway, jumping into my mind like an unwanted intruder.

If I can't ever have Kyra, what would be so bad about dating Brianna?

Three beers later—or four, maybe—we finished the chemistry homework. For me, beer or not, it was a snap.

Brianna smiled. "For a girl whose heart has been broken, I'm doing a good job of hiding how much I'm hurt, aren't I?"

Music was playing now. Soft music. I couldn't remember her turning on the stereo.

"Very good job," I said.

"And you're doing a good job too." She patted my knee. "Don't look surprised. Of course I know about you and Kyra. Everyone does. Most of the girls think it's sweet, how much you adore her."

"They do?" I asked.

"I think she's too stupid to realize what a good thing she could have if she started dating you."

I laughed. In my ears, it sounded hollow.

Brianna leaned forward and kissed my forehead. "I think you're sweet."

"What about Hale . . . ?"

He's your best friend, an inner voice told me.

Brianna took one of my hands and slapped the back of it. Gently. "Bad boy. Don't talk about Hale anymore. He's in the past."

"But . . ."

"In the past. And . . ." Brianna pushed some hair away from her face. Beautiful blonde hair. Like Kyra's. ". . . more than once Hale said he thought you and I should go out. He thought your brains and my looks . . ."

Brianna stood, flipping her hair back over her shoulders. "More beer?"

I felt reckless. Strong. "Yeah."

But she came back with more than beer. She carried the beer, one can stacked on the other, in her right hand. Her left hand was closed.

"Let's have some fun." Her voice was low and throaty. "My parents are gone for the weekend."

My heart was racing. "Fun?"

She opened her left hand, palm up. In her hand were two small white pills. "Fun," she repeated. "This stuff is really fun."

She sat beside me and snuggled, her head on my shoulder. "Take one. They're not drugs. They're prescription pills. Roofies. Make you feel like you're floating."

"Roofies," I repeated.

She sat straight. Popped one in her mouth. "Like

that. I wouldn't take them if they were bad for a person."

Then she leaned forward, placing one hand on my jaw. It felt cool. She'd been holding a can of beer in that hand. She brought her other hand forward and placed the pill on my lip.

I could hardly breathe. The smell of her perfume was all over me. The softness of her hands. Her eyes, up close and staring into mine. Her lips, like she was just about to kiss me. The music.

I opened my mouth a little.

She slipped the pill inside, then leaned back again and handed me the beer. "You're going to love this," she said. "Drink."

I did.

■   ■   ■

Soon my muscles lost their tightness and my mind began to float. I smiled.

"See," she said, "now you're relaxed. I've never seen you relaxed. Always your brain working too hard."

"Too hard," I repeated.

"Like you're always trying to figure things out. Just let life drift by, Tyrone. With me."

She held my hand and intertwined her fingers with mine.

"Drift by," I repeated. "With you."

She put her other arm around my shoulders and settled against me. "Isn't the fire beautiful?"

"Beautiful." I giggled. "Like you."

Time stopped having any meaning.

I drifted. And drifted.

The flames of the fire seemed to melt into each other, and it became a big, wonderful glow.

And that's all I can remember.

■   ■   ■

Except for the next morning.

When I woke up on the couch. In my jeans. With my shirt on the coffee table, on top of her homework. With bright sunlight hurting my eyes.

And Brianna asleep beside me, under the blanket that we shared.

I eased away from her. I was thirsty. I went to the bathroom and looked in the mirror. Saw lipstick smeared across my forehead. Then I saw movement beside me.

Brianna was at the doorway.

"Tyrone," she said, "I have a feeling we'd better not tell anyone about last night."

I nodded. My head throbbed.

"And Tyrone," she said, her forehead crinkled, "I did have fun. But I'm not sure I'm ready to get that serious with you. Is that okay?"

Since I couldn't remember anything after the fire had become a wonderful glow, I nodded again.

But why did my soul feel like it had just been discarded by her?

And by me?

26

"Coming to church?" Gran asked. She glanced up at me from over a cup of tea at the kitchen table.

This was the question she asked me every Sunday. In a nice, nonthreatening way.

Since I'd just stepped in the door, I'd been dreading her first question. On this Sunday, after being gone all night, I'd expected her to break the weekly routine and ask me about that instead.

"Church . . ." I said, my voice trailing.

"Church. White building. Tall steeple. Hymns." She scratched her forehead in a fake, theatrical way. "Almost forgot. And God. Remember? Creator of the universe? The One who loves you?"

I couldn't help but smile. That God. Gran loved reminding me that she believed God was love. My father, on the other hand, believed that God was very concerned with financial matters. Specifically my *father's* financial matters.

"Maybe next Sunday," I answered. It was my usual answer. Better than saying no.

I took a half step toward my bedroom. I still expected her to ask where I'd been. I didn't want to lie, but I didn't want to tell the truth.

"Sure," she said. "Next Sunday."

I was at the hallway before she spoke again.

"Tyrone."

I froze but didn't turn.

"Anytime you want to talk," she continued, "I'm here to listen."

"Thanks, Gran," I said in a cheery voice that I didn't feel. "That's good to know."

■ ■ ▧

Monday morning the faint honk of Hale's car reached me in the kitchen of Gran's apartment.

I took my bowl of soggy bran flakes, drained the milk into the sink, and threw the rest into the garbage can. I'd been staring at the bran flakes for about 20 minutes, hoping that Hale wouldn't stop by like he did every morning.

He honked again.

I sighed and grabbed my backpack.

How was I going to look my best friend in the eye after spending time with his ex-girlfriend on the day he'd broken up with her?

All Sunday I'd felt guilty just thinking about it.

I wondered if I should confess to Hale before he heard about it from someone else. But who would he hear it from? Brianna had told me to keep it a secret. Was she going to blab to the world? If nobody was going to know except for me and Brianna, then Hale wasn't going to find out.

So was I considering a confession to Hale to make *me* feel better? And if that was true, maybe I shouldn't say anything to him, in case he'd feel horrible.

My mind was spinning, just as it had all of Sunday.

Hale honked a third time.

"Bye, Gran!" I shouted.

I shut the door behind me and walked slowly down the apartment steps.

Would Hale see it in my eyes as I got into the Camaro?

I opened the car door.

"Hey, bud," he said. "Missed you Saturday night. Good weekend?"

Was he testing me?

"Average," I answered. Thinking, *Except for cuddling up in front of a fire with your ex-girlfriend.*

"Backseat," he said as I slid in the front on the shotgun side. "One more person joining us. And much as I like you, buddy, she's got a lot more to offer." Hale laughed.

Another girlfriend? I didn't say anything. Just crawled in the back.

Hale took off with his usual neck-snapping acceleration. Then braked two blocks later with equal deceleration.

In front of Brianna's house.

She sauntered down the sidewalk.

Brianna?

"Didn't you guys break up?" I asked Hale.

He turned down the radio. "What's that?"

Brianna was halfway to the Camaro.

"You and Brianna. Didn't you break up?"

Hale laughed. "Wishful thinking, buddy. I know you've got your eye on her. Don't blame you, of course. Beauty like that. But she's all mine. And I love her. We had a good talk on Sunday and got everything straightened out."

He jumped from the Camaro, ran around the front of the hood, and opened the door for her.

At the side of the car, with the door still open, Brianna arched up beside Hale and threw her arms around his neck. She kissed him deeply.

As she slid into the front seat, with Hale walking around the front of the Camaro, Brianna turned her head and smiled at me.

"Hope you're good at keeping secrets," she whispered. "Guess Hale wasn't done with me after all." She winked and blew me a kiss.

Since Sunday morning, waking up at Brianna's, I hadn't believed I could hate myself any more than I did.

But at that moment, I realized there was still a ways to go with that self-hatred.

Even if I didn't know then what I know now.

(now)

"Good name, in man and woman, . . . is the
immediate jewel of their souls."

Othello, Act III, Scene 3

It's Thursday afternoon. The day after
tomorrow will be two weeks since Sammy died.
A week ago I did a drug deal, going with Hale to
deliver pharmaceuticals to Miranda. Even though
I mostly sat on the couch, I was there. I was a part
of it. And I began to wonder if this is really what
I want for my life. Monday of this week began with
a trip to the police station. Tuesday I learned from
Brianna that my best friend had betrayed me as
badly as I'd betrayed him.

I'm at the bottom of the pit.

I've had all day Wednesday to think about
whether I want to remain there.

I've had all day Wednesday to consider Gran's
advice. I could still hear her words: *"You don't have*

to make yourself right to approach God, but approach him, and he will make you right." All the God talk and a "religious life" hadn't worked out very well for my father. But Gran was different, and I wanted to know why.

So now I'm about to try it for myself.

■   ■   ■

I find Mitch in the back of his bike shop, tightening spokes on a fancy mountain bike.

"Hey," he says, giving me his famous grin.

I let the grin bounce off me.

"I'm done," I say.

"Done?"

"Done pretending that it's okay to take money for what I've been doing for you."

He straightens and sets his spoke wrench down. Mitch arches an eyebrow. "You're suggesting . . ."

"Little white pills. Roofies. Ecstasy. Blue pills, white pills, orange pills."

Mitch wipes the grease off his hands. He faces me, looking amused. "What indignation. You certainly sound a lot more knowledgeable than I would have guessed."

"Hale let me in on it," I say.

"Good, good. It was about time you moved up the chain."

"So Hale knew from the beginning." The words come hard for me.

"He's a lot more street-smart than you," Mitch says. "After the first delivery, he told me he knew what was in the package. Said if he was going to do something like that, he didn't want to be caught blind. Which was fine with me. I also needed someone to move it from the packages to the customers. Hale does a great job."

"Did," I say. "He's gone too."

"I'll miss him," Mitch says without sincerity. He picks up the spoke wrench and begins tightening spokes again, his back half turned to me.

"But you told us it was multilevel marketing," I argue. "Vitamins and health stuff. You said you were looking for a way to keep the IRS from knowing you made extra money on the side. Why didn't you tell us the truth?"

Mitch laughs. "People believe what they want to believe. You took that first hundred dollars from me so fast it was like you were a starving dog reaching for a bone. No matter what story I gave you, you would have told yourself it was true, just to keep getting the money."

He's right. I can't deny it. And I have a Ford Escort to show for it.

"So what got to your conscience?" Mitch prods. "Why the questions now?"

"I'm through," I repeat.

He shrugs. "Whatever."

That wasn't the reaction I expected.

"And Hale?" Mitch asks, in the same cool manner. "Is he coming back?"

"What he does is his business."

Again, laughter from Mitch. But this time there was an edge to it. "Yeah, I heard that he had a *discussion* with you before he left town. He talked and you listened. Right?"

I can't deny that either. And I'll never forget that night . . .

■ ■ ■

On the Friday night after Sammy died, it would have been his eighteenth birthday. There was a party for Kyra at the church.

It seemed that all of the life had been sucked out of everybody in Macon. Me included.

I was haunted by my memories of the night that Sammy died, and my guilt at my part in it. Because of that, it seemed that all my longings for Kyra had shriveled. That Friday night, when I thought of her, it was with sympathy. And of course, guilt.

Her twin brother. Dead.

There was no way I was going to attend the party.

First of all, it was at a church. Second, I felt like everyone there would stare at me all night with laser-vision hatred and anger. I expected, then, that it would become just another inconsequential Friday night.

How wrong I was.

From my bedroom shortly after 8 P.M. I heard someone outside yelling my name.

I looked out my apartment window and saw Hale Ramsey leaning against my car. Because of the streetlight, I could see he had a baseball bat.

"Tyrone Larson!" he shouted again. "Tyrone Larson!"

It did occur to me that the bat in Hale Ramsey's hands could be a weapon. I wondered who he wanted to fight. Because he was my best friend, I knew I needed to go with him and stand beside him no matter who he intended to battle. And, at the very least, try to talk him out of going hillbilly with rage on whoever he'd chosen as a target. Over the past couple of weeks Hale had been unstable, and his mood swings had worsened considerably since Sammy's death.

I threw on a jacket and hurried out the door, grateful that Gran was already asleep.

"Hey!" I called out to Hale as I hurried down the sidewalk leading away from the apartment building.

At my voice, he spun from staring up at my apartment window to face me squarely. He watched in silence as I approached.

I smiled. "Bit early in the season for the batting cage, isn't it?"

"Nope." He bit the word off coldly. His face, lost in shadow, was unreadable.

The dragon deep inside my belly with its coils of self-hatred—the beast I'd been trying to conquer since the night I betrayed Hale with Brianna—stirred and rumbled. My remorse and anguish were as fresh as they were on the morning I'd left her house with such shame. Was I finally going to pay for what I'd hidden from him?

"You might remember," he said slowly, "one night in the Camaro when we followed Brianna and Mitchell Wade in his Porsche."

I nodded. Yes, I was going to pay. In a way, I welcomed it. The burden had been so heavy for so long.

"And you might recall how I said that if the one person I trusted like a brother ever let me down, I'd be gone."

"Hale . . ." I stopped. There was nothing I could say to defend myself.

"I'm on my way back to Hazard County. No matter how bad it's going to be there, it will be a long sight better than staying here." He lifted his bat. "You deserve this for what you did to me. Are you going to deny that?"

I remained silent.

He swung. With icy fury. The bat whistled past my head and came down on the rear window of my Escort.

The thud was surprisingly muted. The glass of my rear window formed a spiderweb of cracks, with a white core at the center of impact.

"Deny it," Hale said. "Please."

Strangely, I thought of Jesus in front of Pontius Pilate. All Jesus had needed to do was speak one word in his defense, and Pilate was prepared to free him from death on the cross. But Jesus was innocent.

I was not. Anything I said would proclaim my guilt.

And coward that I was, I remained silent.

The bat came down again.

And again.

And again.

Hale began sobbing as he smashed my rear window into tiny pieces that sprayed the backseat.

Then he beat the rear fenders. And the trunk, making dents all over the body of my car.

If he had been hitting me, I would be dead.

Finally, exhausted, he quit. "Deny it," he said again. But in a broken voice.

I wanted to.

Oh, I wanted so badly to be able to deny it.

But I could not.

He lifted his eyes to mine.

I looked away.

"That's it, then," he said. "If I ever see you again, I believe I'll kill you."

Then he walked.

Mitch probably sees it in my face, the pain of the memory of what happened that night with Hale.

"Word gets around," Mitch says. "Got hit by a hailstorm, huh?"

Unlike Detective Sanders, who may not have known she was making a pun when she asked me about my car, Mitch laughs at his own cleverness.

"Listen," Mitch says. "Don't blame yourself. Everybody tries fooling themselves. Look at your friend Hale. He wanted his eyes wide open about what he was doing for me, but didn't dare ask himself why Brianna started going out with him just after he started dealing the pills."

I feel like I am gaping at Mitch.

Mitch shakes his head. "See what I mean about

people choosing to believe what they want to believe? Hale didn't dare admit to himself that Brianna was using him to get her supply of pills. Hale's big mistake was to finally tell her where he was getting them. I'd warned him from the beginning to keep it quiet. But no, he tells her and she decides to come running to me. Wanted to go straight to the source. I was happy to help her. But only after we had a little discussion, and she was willing to make a deal of her own."

I think about the night that Hale and I saw her drive out of town in his Porsche.

"We followed you that night," I say, wanting to confirm my guess.

"Didn't do you much good, did it? One little call on my cell phone about a driver weaving on the road behind me, and the troopers had you pulled over in minutes."

"Sammy *died*. Don't you care about that?"

For a moment, darkness crosses Mitch's face. "More than you know. He was a good kid."

"More than I know." I repeat his words, spitting them out. "You're the one who brought this stuff into town. You're the one who—"

"If not me, someone else. I'm not trying to justify what I did. It made me money. I wish he hadn't died. But it could have just as easily been someone else bringing the stuff in. And no one made him take it. That he did on his own."

"You're right. Let the blame fall where it should." I turn to walk out.

Mitch moves faster than I anticipate. He grabs

my shoulder and spins me around. With his eyes, he searches my face, as if trying to read my thoughts. "No threats?" he says.

"How can I threaten you? I picked up packages addressed to someone else. If I went to the cops, it would be your word against mine that you gave me all that cash. Hale's not around to go to the cops to tell them what was in the packages, and you probably know as well as I do that he's going to hide in the hills and never be found. I came here today because I just wanted to tell you that I was done with the deliveries. For good."

Mitch keeps searching my face. "Ty–"

For the first time since I've known Mitch, I hear a threat in his voice.

"Who are they going to believe?" he continues in a low, controlled tone. "A well-respected teacher, or a kid whose dad is in jail? If I go down, you go down."

That's when I realize. Yes, there's a threat in his voice, but something else too. . . .

Fear. Like this is the first time Mitch has ever really been cornered. Like finally something has cracked his cool. Like finally he's no longer just the catalyst. That Sammy's death has impacted him too. And he's scared. Enough to maybe even turn mean.

"I know," is all I say, knowing I need to get out of there. And fast.

And I do know.

As I walk out of Mitch's bike shop, I know I'm trapped. Doing what I have to do isn't going to be easy.

I know that if I tell the truth, I'll go down.

But what about Sammy?

(then)

"To thine own self be true;
and it must follow, as the night the day,
thou canst not then be false to any man."

Hamlet, Act I, Scene 3

On Wednesday, three days before Sammy died, Hale and I were walking down the hallway together from math class to the library.

At Macon High, in front of the administration office, is a lobby where all the school trophies are stored behind glass. This is where Brianna stood with Sammy.

Well, more than just stood. She was basically draped all over him. And they were talking and laughing.

Hale saw this at the same time I did, as we rounded the corner.

He stopped. In shock.

Other students passed us, headed in both directions. There was the usual loud buzz of scattered conversations. Nothing to indicate that Hale's world as he knew it had just come to an end.

"Ty," Hale said, "is that . . . is that . . ." He began to march toward them.

I followed.

When Hale stopped in front of Sammy and Brianna, Sammy grinned as if nothing was wrong. I could see that he didn't have his arm around Bri, just the other way around. But I'd have bet a thousand bucks Hale didn't see it that way.

Sammy opened his mouth, but then shut it when Hale demanded, "What's going on?" loud enough that conversations around us dropped.

"What's it look like?" Brianna tossed her hair and tightened her right arm around Sammy's waist. "You and me are through, Hale Ramsey."

"Uh, Bri—" Sammy began again.

"Bri?" Hale echoed, speaking to Sammy. "Bri? Like suddenly she's your girl? What kind of slimy snake are you?"

"Hale, this isn't what it looks like." Sammy explained.

This time Brianna interrupted Sammy. "Go away, hillbilly," Brianna told Hale. "I'm tired of you."

Hale's anger fizzled. He turned to me, and I saw bewilderment and pain in his face. "Ty . . ."

I had no answer.

The night before, Hale and Brianna had left the school together, holding hands as they walked into the parking lot toward Hale's Camaro. It was Brianna's birthday. The night he'd said he would propose to her. And he had. He had just been starting to tell me the details when we'd happened upon the scene in the hallway.

"Go away," Brianna repeated to Hale.

"Baby," Hale said, pleading. I'd never seen him like this before. Slack. Drooped. None of the angry pride that always sustained him. "But what about the ring that you and me picked out last—"

"We're through," Brianna said. "Can't you get that into your thick hillbilly skull?"

"But . . . but why?" Hale was miserable and angry and totally confused.

"Come on," I said. "Someone tell me what's going on."

"This is none of your business," Brianna said. "Not even Hale's business. Not anymore. He and I have nothing to talk about. As of now—"

"Walk away from her," Hale hissed at Sammy. "I don't know what you're trying to pull, but walk away. Now. Before it's too late. I respect you enough to give you that chance."

Now, not only had all conversation around us ended, but most people in the hallway had stopped.

Hale brought up his fists. "Git," he told Sammy.

"Hale . . ." Sammy appeared slightly bewildered. The tone of his voice was placating. "Come on. You know I wouldn't—"

"Last chance," Hale said. "Walk."

"What are you going to do?" Brianna taunted Hale.

Hale swung. Hard.

Sammy shifted, just enough to slip the punch.

Hale's momentum took his fist into the glass of the trophy case directly behind Sammy.

He punched through, smashing the glass and

scattering shards in all directions. In the silence of the lobby, the loudness was as startling as the quickness with which it had happened.

Hale pulled his fist back. Blood streamed from the knuckles.

Both he and Sammy stared at his bloody fist, as if neither could comprehend what had happened.

Brianna, however, smiled—the kind of smile I'd never seen on Kyra's face. Like she had caused the pain and was now enjoying it.

"Come on," she said, removing her arm from Sammy's waist. "Let's go." She tugged at his arm.

"But . . ." Sammy didn't follow her. He opened his mouth, as if to try to explain again.

"What's going on?" came a voice from the doorway of the administrative office.

Mrs. Wilcox. Our principal.

Until that moment the lobby had been like a still-life scene. Dozens of students, frozen in place, all watching the drama.

With her voice, motion began again. Students suddenly began walking.

"What's going on?" Mrs. Wilcox nearly shouted.

She was powerless, however, against the mass of students, all determined to flee, including Brianna, who had grabbed Sammy's hand and pulled him into motion too.

The only person who could not escape was Hale. The blood dripping onto the floor at his feet was evidence too powerful.

"Hale Ramsey," Mrs. Wilcox barked. "Andrew Hale Ramsey, what have you done?"

It was an indication of how badly Brianna had broken Hale's spirit that he meekly allowed Mrs. Wilcox to grab him by the elbow.

"Hale–," I began.

"Enough from you for now," Mrs. Wilcox said to me. "You get a janitor. Hale and I are going to have a discussion as soon as we wrap his hand." She turned to Hale. "And you'd better have a great explanation. Understand?"

My last view of Hale that afternoon was of him vainly peering over his shoulder for any sight of Brianna as Mrs. Wilcox, maintaining that firm grip on his elbow, marched him down the hallway.

The night of the play?

Like an idiot, I had a flask with me. One of
Hale's. A moonshine flask, he called it, refusing to
tell me exactly what was in it. I'd taken a sip and
felt my choking breaths outward had the flames of
a dragon. He'd nodded with satisfaction, as if that's
exactly how he liked it.

Hale had wandered away, and I'd gone backstage,
sharing the flask with anyone who cared.

Including Miranda.

She was in a strange mood, and I figured it was
jitters for the play. Whatever the reason, she didn't
mind a couple of sips from the flask. I'd offered it to
Sammy, who declined.

Miranda teased him about it, and I could tell by

Sammy's face that once again he felt like a Goody Two-shoes around the woman he adored.

Then the lights went down in the auditorium, and I slipped back to my seat.

I didn't see Sammy until after the play. "You looked bummed out," I told him.

Most of the crowd had dispersed. The echoes of the congratulations had faded.

"Yeah," he said. "I am."

"Come on," I answered. "You were great."

We stood in the hallway outside the gym.

Sammy waited for a couple pairs of parents to leave, and when it was relatively private again, he spoke. "Kyra, man. She's bumming me out."

"You too, huh?" I wanted to say. But didn't.

"She . . ." He struggled to find the words. "Mom's been missing some prescription pills, you know. Turns out the thief was Kyra."

"Kyra!"

He nodded. "Perfect Kyra. The one who gets all the attention. Tonight too. I mean, she deserved it."

Which was true. The lead role. Except for a little obvious nervousness early, she'd been flawless.

"That's part of what bums me out," he said. "She's my twin. She's so good she deserves the attention. Even when she's messing up with those pills, she's that good. So what's she doing taking drugs? Me . . ." He struggled for words again. "Well, I'm just Sammy. The guy on the sidelines. Mr. Invisible."

He let that hang.

I was in shock. This guy was a top jock who was

liked by everyone. And one of the star basketball players. And he felt the same way I did? No way was this guy invisible!

"Reminds me," I said to break the tension. "There was a receptionist for a psychiatrist. She buzzes the doctor and says, 'There's a man here in the waiting room who says he's invisible.' "

I stopped.

Sammy looked up. "And?"

"Doctor says to the receptionist, 'Tell him I can't see him right now.' "

"You're weird," Sammy said with no hint of a grin.

"Thanks," I said. "And you're determined to stay in a bad mood."

When Sammy continued, I could hear the sadness in his voice. "You weren't there, backstage, when Miranda and I finished our roles as Celia and Oliver and were waiting for the rest of the play to end. When I was Mr. Invisible again."

"You're never Mr. Invisible," I said. "You—"

"To Miranda I am. Behind the curtains, while the play continued, she gave me this big kiss on the cheek. I'm guessing just because she was happy that we'd survived onstage. I wanted it to be a kiss because she likes me the way I like her."

"Hey," I said. "A kiss is a kiss."

I didn't say the rest of what I was thinking: *If your sister, Kyra, ever kissed me, I wouldn't care why.*

"I guess so," Sammy said. "She invited me to her party tonight."

"What's wrong with that?"

I was thinking, *If Kyra ever invited me to a party* . . .

"Nothing's wrong with it. But I don't want to be just a friend. She thinks I need to lighten up."

"Lighten up then."

"It's just that she and I are different."

"I think she likes you," I said. "As more than a friend. I think there's only one solution."

"What's that?"

"Let's go to Miranda's party. Take a chance and find out exactly where the adventure will lead you."

He grinned with sudden resolve. "Done."

How I wish I'd never given him that advice.

The night that Sammy died?

It was a chaotic party. At Miranda's house.

Naturally I was looking through and among all the people there for Kyra.

There was a real buzz to this party. I think because of the play. Mitchell Wade's play. It had ended about an hour earlier. It went great. I sat in the darkness, unable to take my eyes off Kyra the entire time she performed.

Here at Miranda's the play was all that anyone seemed to be talking about.

Cigarette smoke filled the house. I smelled spilled beer. The music was loud and it made everyone talk at a near shout. Waving in the corner caught my eye.

Sammy James.

I pointed at my chest. *Me?* I mouthed it.

He nodded. Waved me toward him.

I moved toward him, squeezing past clusters of people.

"Hey!" Sammy shouted in my ear. He held a can of beer. Unusual. "See, I can lighten up with the best of them!"

I nodded in reply. I felt out of place at the party. Hale had a reason for being here. He wanted to talk to Brianna and try to convince her to go out with him again. Sammy was here because of Miranda. I could try to fool myself into thinking I was here because of Kyra, but it was getting harder and harder to do that. "Anytime, now," I said, "she'll be here to throw herself into your arms."

"What?"

Sammy hadn't heard me above the party noise. Good thing.

Miranda had just walked to the center of the room. But her eyes weren't on Sammy. They were on Mitch.

"Nothing," I said loudly. Miranda took Mitch's hand and began to dance with him. With luck, Sammy would continue to speak to me and not turn and notice.

But luck wasn't with us. Sammy half turned and saw Miranda. Laughing. With Mitch.

He stared at them for at least a full minute, then turned back to me. Looking like someone had just dropped a sandbag on his head. He glanced at his beer. Gulped it.

His eyes darted. "Any chance you can find me an aspirin? I've got a killer headache."

I shrugged.

"Come on," he said. "Help me out. I'm not feeling so balanced. Don't know if I can walk to the end of the room. Get me an aspirin."

I shrugged again. Forced my way back through clusters of partiers. Waited at the bathroom door until it opened. Found a bottle of aspirin. Took a couple. Forced my way back to Sammy. True to his word, he was still there. Swaying slightly. His face was flushed. That's when I figured he had to have drunk more than one beer already.

"She promised me that tonight would be special," he said, gulping two aspirin with a mouthful of beer, "At the play. When she kissed me. That's why I'm here. Drinking beer."

I felt his pain.

Really.

Love can be such a bummer.

"Now look," he shouted. "She's gone to Mitch. And Mitch . . ." Sammy's eyes were glassy. "Mitch. Man, I poured my heart out to him about her. He of all people should know that my heart is breaking to see him make the moves on her."

As if on cue, Mitch smiled at Sammy.

Accident? Or deliberate. Did Mitch know what Sammy was thinking?

"I thought if I came here, tonight might just be the night," Sammy continued. "That I could finally tell Miranda that I love her." His speech was now slurring slightly. "That I'd know just what to say, like Celia and Oliver, to make her fall into my arms."

"Sammy . . ."

He seemed to be working hard at concentrating. "But it doesn't look that way. She's having too much fun dancing with Mitch to hang out with me. To her I'm just a guy who shoots hoops with her. A *friend.*"

He stopped, drew in his breath, and put a hand to his forehead. "Is it hot in here to you?"

I shook my head. Sammy—square, good guy Sammy—was getting drunk. And I knew why. I felt that kind of pain every time I looked at Kyra and knew she'd gone out with another guy.

"You know what?" Sammy said suddenly. His grin had become wide and loose. "I don't think I even care anymore about Miranda. Do you believe me?"

I shook my head.

He leaned into me. His breath was an odd mixture of sweetness with the bitterness of beer.

"So this is the dark side, buddy." Sammy was slurring more. "The dark side always calls. And I think I always wanted to know. What's so great about alcohol? about drugs? Why do kids do it? So I went ahead. Gave it a try."

He tried to straighten. "Got to tell you, Ty. Flying a little right now. Don't think I'll do it again, but I'll never forget what it's like to fly." Sammy's brow crinkled. "What exactly were we talking about?"

I shrugged. Didn't want to remind him that Miranda was dancing with Mitch, almost within arm's reach.

"Thirsty," Sammy said. "Need water."

But he wasn't talking to me. Just talking.

"Bye." He waved without looking at me and staggered toward the kitchen. "Need water."

I hoped Hale wasn't still angry at Sammy. But I knew he still hadn't forgotten that scene with Sammy and Brianna in the Macon High hallway by the trophy case. It had earned Hale a day's suspension from school. Even though Sammy had tried to approach Hale two days later to tell him nothing was going on between him and Brianna, Hale hadn't really believed Sammy. Tonight Hale, Sammy, and Brianna were all at the party. I knew that Sammy better not even talk to Brianna or he'd be in trouble. In the condition he was in now, he wouldn't stand a chance in a fight against Hale.

I moved to a corner and stood there. Alone.

No sign of Kyra.

Yet.

I stood alone for about 20 minutes.

A couple of times I glanced over at Sammy, who had returned from the kitchen and was now on the couch, sleeping off his beer. I shook my head and smiled sadly for him. First time taking drugs. He wasn't going to enjoy the next morning. That I knew from experience. I hoped he wouldn't hate himself for it as much as I had.

I'd just about given up hope that Kyra would show when she came running through the apartment, screaming for Sammy. I figured she must have been somewhere, drinking or doing drugs herself, the way she was yelling. She was really hysterical.

She ran over to the couch. She knew. Somehow she knew before any of us. Maybe it was the twin thing or something.

Sammy was dead. He died right there on the couch. And all because I didn't know then what I know now.

(now)

"To thee I do commend my watchful soul,
ere I let fall the windows of mine eyes:
sleeping and waking, O, defend me still."

Richard III, Act V, Scene 3

It's Friday afternoon. Tomorrow will be two weeks since Sammy died. A week ago my best friend beat my car with a baseball bat and threatened to kill me if he ever saw me again. And yesterday I took my first steps at owning up to my responsi-bilities in all of this.

Now I'm on an interstate somewhere in Indiana.

I'd gone to school, but could think of nothing else but what I needed to do.

A half hour before noon, I'd mentally reviewed my financial situation and decided that I might barely be able to afford to do what I wanted to do.

At 11:45, when the bell rang, I'd marched out of school, stepped into my snot-green Escort, and driven out of the parking lot with the plastic sheet in the rear window flapping in the breeze.

And I'd been right about the mildew smell.
Although the rain had long stopped since my meeting with Brianna, my backseat was still soaked. And
it wasn't pleasant to breathe.

From the parking lot I'd swung past a service
station. Emptied my bank account through the ATM
and loaded up with Dr Pepper and Doritos. Then
I'd headed south and east at five miles an hour over
the speed limit, with the wind howling through the
plastic sheet at the back of my car.

Two o'clock found me south of the Indiana
border. Thinking about Sammy. About Hale. About
God. Now, as I drive, my thoughts begin to swirl
together.

I think again of my mother, who hadn't had a
chance. But who had taken a chance so I could have
a chance. And what had I done with her sacrifice?
Would she be happy to know that the son she'd
given her life for had been part of drug deals? part
of a friend's death?

And then, seemingly out of nowhere, I remember
Gran's words about all the men—great men—who
had still needed God's forgiveness. Who had felt
so guilty for what they'd done in committing one
of the greatest sins possible. Who couldn't change
on their own.

They needed hope. They needed Jesus.

But then there was my dad, who'd had Jesus.
Who'd worn Jesus like a suit of clothes and then
had acted a totally different way. Who'd stolen
money from little kids. Who'd betrayed not only
his organization, but our family. What little trust

I'd had for him as a kid had been completely shattered the day he went to prison. I hadn't answered any of his letters or phone calls since.

But now I knew my father didn't have the corner on betrayal. I'd betrayed Hale, my friend, by spending the night with Brianna—right after they broke up. And I'd betrayed myself by looking the other way when Hale and I went to pick up the "vitamins." I mean, I wasn't stupid. But I, too—just like my father—had been looking for the "quick way," the "easy way" to make money.

As the wind continues to howl around the car, I'm tempted to pull over. To put my head in my hands and sob. Where no one could see me.

Instead I stubbornly keep going. But a groan escapes me. The kind of groan that comes from deep inside—that place where no one knows you're hurting. For the first time, it hits me. I'm as bad as my father. And I've fallen into the same trap.

No, I'm worse. At least my dad hadn't killed people. But the drugs—of which I was a part—had killed Sammy James. One of my friends. The guy who had played go-between when Hale and I had been at war with the jocks. He'd deserved better.

But I had betrayed Sammy. First, by helping bring drugs to Macon—drugs that killed him. And then by not being his friend enough to get him help, to stay with him at that party. I would forever feel those degrees of guilt.

Now there was only one thing I could do for Sammy: Tell the truth myself, and ask Hale the question I had to ask him. The question that had been growing in my mind ever since Hale had disappeared from Macon that Friday night, after beating my car with a baseball bat.

■   ■   ■

I watch the land go from flat to rounded, then hilly.

Semi after semi passes me, the back draft from each one sucking at my Escort and wobbling me from side to side within my lane.

I'm anxious for it to get dark.

At night, state troopers won't notice my rear window. I'm afraid that the lack of visibility it affords me is breaking any number of safety regulations. And that if a trooper calls in my tag and driver's license, the trooper will discover that I'm wanted in an investigation into the death of a bright 18-year-old named Sammy James.

I have a long ways to go to reach Hazard County.

And I can't stop thinking.

I feel the lowest I've ever felt. Just like the prodigal son.

I'd been rolling my eyes when Gran made me read that story from her Bible, but now the words come back to me. My mother had given me a chance at life, a chance that took away her own life, and I've "squandered" it. Now I, just like that prodigal son, am at rock-bottom. I need help. But I'm also afraid. Is what I've done so bad that God won't want me anymore?

Then I remember the prodigal story again. That the prodigal returned home, wondering what his father would say. And he got a totally different reception than he thought he'd get! His father had even hugged him.

Could it be like that for me with God? Like it was for Gran? I wonder.

Is God waiting for me, just as the prodigal's father waited for him?

Waiting for me to acknowledge the sacrifice of his Son's life for me? Just as I had finally acknowledged my mother's sacrifice to give me life?

Is now the time?

■　　■　　■

About midnight, I cross the Kentucky line.

I fight sleep for about the next hour. I do this by sticking my arm out the window. It's cold outside, and the wind at 70 miles an hour is even worse. I hold my arm outside until it's numb. Then I reach under my shirt and pinch myself with those frozen fingers. The shock of ice against my skin jolts me from drowsiness for five minutes or so. Then I start the process again.

I don't dare question the sanity of what I'm doing. I just have to know the answer to my burning question. For me. For Sammy.

Did Hale give Sammy the drug that killed him?

And then the follow-up question begs to be asked: If Hale did give Sammy the Ecstasy, was it just to make money, or because he wanted revenge for that day in the school hallway when Brianna betrayed him?

I also know I have to come clean with Hale—
to tell him what really happened between Brianna
and me.

I think about some of the Roman generals as they
invaded Britain. When they landed, they ordered
the boats burned. The soldiers knew then that there
would be no retreat, and it forced them to fight with
much more intensity.

I have no boats to burn, but I do know that I am
well past the halfway mark. At this point, I don't
have enough money to turn around and buy the fuel
it would take for me to get back to Macon. My only
hope, slim as it is, lies in Hazard County.

Land of Kentucky boxing gloves. Because that's
how people there fight, according to Hale. With
switchblades.

I wonder if I'll be able to find him. And if I do,
how exactly I'm going to ask the question. And how
exactly I'm going to say what I need to say.

I know only God can give me the strength to do
what I need to do.

■　　■　　■

At four in the morning, I calculate that I have only
a couple hours left to drive. I am exhausted. I definitely don't want to arrive in Hazard in darkness.

I decide to pull over at the next rest stop. As
soon as I am parked, I lean my head back against
the seat.

I don't remember falling asleep, it happens so
quickly.

When I wake, it's because I'm cold.

I check my watch. Two hours have passed.

Which means I'll get to Hazard around eight.

This is good.

I have driven most of the way in darkness so I didn't have to worry so much about a state trooper spotting my rear window. But after all these hours of highway driving, the plastic is shredded and nearly gone. I'm sure it will look suspicious.

This close to my destination—and with so little money left—I'm terrified of what might happen if I'm stopped by a state trooper.

And even more terrified of what might happen in Hazard.

■　　■　　■

Hazard—the town with the same name as the county—seems very much like the way Hale described it to me many times.

Steep hills covered with trees. Other steep hills totally stripped bare by mining. Hazard is a smudged town, grimy from coal dust. It is also a small town. Much smaller than Macon.

I stop in front of Ned's Café.

I walk in, and all eyes turn in my direction. Three tables are occupied. By old men smoking cigarettes and squinting at me in suspicion. I decide if I don't act now, I'll never act at all.

I pretend I own the town. "Anyone here know Hale Ramsey?" I ask loudly.

Silence greets my question.

(margin text, vertical) tyrone's story

"Fine then," I say. Still loudly. "I'll have a coffee. And wait. Hale smashed in my back window with a baseball bat and I'm here to talk to him about it."

Sure enough, I don't even finish my coffee before one of the old men in faded coveralls rises and leaves.

If Hazard is anything like Macon, he's gone to tell someone about the kid who marched in and made the announcement about Hale Ramsey. That someone will tell someone else. And so on.

My bet is it will take less than an hour for word of my arrival to reach Hale. Or someone who knows where he is.

As for any other predictions, I have no idea what will happen after that.

33

I'm on my fourth cup of coffee. Every sip is like poison. But it gives me an excuse to stall. Thirty minutes earlier, I finished my breakfast of pancakes and sausage. I've read the local paper and there's nothing to do now except stare at the grimy, fly-specked window that overlooks the main street of Hazard.

I dread the moment that I've got to get up and go to the till and pay my bill.

For three reasons. I'm hoping Hale will hear I'm in the restaurant and come to see me. So getting up from my chair will be like admitting defeat. Also, I have nowhere else to go. And basically no money left even if I had someplace to go in Hazard.

In fact, I've calculated that I'll have $4.50 left after I pay the bill and leave 15 percent for the pear-shaped waitress with the beehive hairstyle.

I'm afraid it'll get caught in the ceiling fan every time she walks across the restaurant.

So if I get up and leave behind the coffee that tastes like poison, I've admitted defeat, I've got no more plans of what to do next, and next to zero money to head back to Macon.

Life is not good.

The old men in the restaurant have been ignoring me since the first one of their group left.

The waitress is ignoring me too as she snaps her gum and examines her fingernails.

Movement crosses in front of the window.

It's a girl. Well, an older teenager. She is wearing jeans and a black jacket. She stops, turns, and opens the door to the restaurant. A bell rings as she enters.

Without hesitation she moves to my table and sits down opposite me. She appraises me without embarrassment.

It gives me a chance to look at her more closely in return. She's about Kyra's age, but the opposite in appearance. Black hair, not blonde. Long and messy, not primped to perfection. A light sprinkling of freckles where Kyra has a careful foundation of makeup. The jacket is wrinkled and slightly dusty—Kyra makes sure her clothing is immaculate—and, even to my unknowledgeable eyes, the jacket is distinctly out of fashion.

"Hale's waiting for you," she says. In those few words, I hear the hillbilly twang so familiar from Hale. "We'll take my truck. I doubt that your car can make it where we're going. In fact, I'm surprised it made it here."

It's my license plate, of course. Iowa. That's how she knows.

She grins. It's unexpected. And unexpectedly beautiful. "Bet you hate the color of it, don't you? Kind of like snot."

Kyra would never use that word.

I get up, pay the bill, and follow her outside.

My car is parked out front, and she stops and marvels at it. At the flapping plastic for a rear window. At the large dimples on the body where Hale took a bat to it.

"My cousin do that?" she snorts.

I nod. "Hale storm."

She groans at the bad pun. But groans in a good way.

"He always did have a temper," she says. "This why he left Iowa in such a hurry? Charges waiting for him on vandalism?"

"It's a little more complicated than that," I say.

"Whatever it is," she says, "you're a brave man to come looking for him. Especially when you show up without a car for him to hit." She gives me a sideways glance. "Because then what else will he have but you?"

Great, I think. But then I remember the two reasons I'm here.

I follow her to an old red pickup that's just as battered as my Escort. But at least it still has a rear window.

I get in. I don't say a word as she starts the engine. And continue to sit quietly as she drives down the main street, out of town, and off the

pavement to a gravel road that leads up into
the hills.

■　　■　　■

It takes 15 minutes of hill-climbing in her truck. The
gravel road gets narrower and narrower until bushes
begin to scrape the sides of the truck. Then the
gravel ends and the road becomes rutted dirt. In
two places she drives through a shallow stream.

She doesn't speak. I'm determined to keep my
mouth shut too.

When she reaches a clearing, she parks and shuts
the motor down. Gets out of the truck. The hinge is
squeaky and sounds loud in the quiet among the
trees.

I get out my side.

The sun is well up by now, and the day is mild.
No clouds. No wind.

The trees are thick and seem ominous with the
shadows that cover the ground. I decide I could get
lost in there in less than five minutes.

"Follow close," she says. "We've got a ways
to go."

"What's your name?" I ask. It seems appropriate
if I have to trust her, I should know her name.

"Wanda," she says. Then she hesitates. "Hale ain't
said much, but I know he's spittin' mad. You sure
you want to go through with this?"

"Not really." I move forward.

She shrugs and leads me to the trees.

To me, it looks like a wall of underbrush ahead.

When we get there, a path seems to magically appear. She steps onto it and almost disappears. I decide I'm going to stay real close.

■　　■　　■

Fifteen or 20 minutes later she stops so suddenly that I almost run into her.

"Walk soft," she says. "Look." She points at the ground.

I don't see anything but leaves and dead branches. "See it?"

Then I do. A large, copper-colored snake with a triangle head. I shrink back.

"Yup," she says. "Copperhead."

Slowly, she leans down, takes a branch, and prods it. With alarming quickness, it slithers under a log.

"More often than not, they're ornery," she says. "They'll want to stay and fight."

"Like a Ramsey?" I ask.

I'm rewarded by another beautiful smile.

"Like a Ramsey."

I expect her to keep moving up the path, but she's staring at the log where the snake disappeared.

"Lots of Ramseys in these parts think I'm crazy," she says. "But I can't get enough of learning about snakes. Or birds. Or anything else that moves. Plenty of Ramseys study animal habits because it's useful for hunting or trapping or fishing. They wouldn't think that's strange. But there's stuff that happens on a cellular level that's absolutely amazing. Even trees have mysteries."

She points at a large oak standing in front of us. "That's maybe 60 feet tall. You have any idea how much water it draws and how much that water weighs? You try moving dozens of gallons 60 feet straight up. An engineering marvel. Scientists can't decide if the tree pulls it up from the top or pushes it up from the bottom."

"I go with osmosis," I say, my mind filled with what I remember from a science article I read three weeks earlier on yet another lonely Friday night. "From what I've read, I've got to believe it's a vacuum that pulls the water upward. Experiments they ran on redwoods in California . . ."

I realize what I'm saying. And that someone finds it interesting.

She stares at me, openmouthed.

I stare back at her.

I think we're each having a moment. A connection moment. Like suddenly there is someone else in the world who thinks the same way.

"Jumping horny toads," she says.

"Yosemite Sam, right?" I'm referring to a Bugs Bunny character.

"Right." Her eyes narrow as if she is seeing me for the first time. "Tell you what. As we walk up the rest of the way, I'll be praying that Hale Ramsey leaves you in enough pieces for me to put together."

"Um," I say, as if seeing her for the first time. "Me too."

Hale is waiting for me at the top of the hill. Well, not a hill. A small mountain. In east Kentucky. Hillbilly country.

On top there is an area of hard rock where no trees can grow. It gives us a view of the entire valley. But this is not a moment to enjoy the view.

Hale is standing beside a large bush that has somehow managed to get a foothold among the smooth, weatherworn rock that forms this knob at the top of the hill.

Wanda is beside me.

"Hale," she says. "Here he is. Go easy on him."

"Good-bye," he replies. "I owe you one for bringing him here."

Just like that, she's gone. Back into the trees below us.

There is only me.

And Hale.

And a hawk, circling high above. At least, I think it's a hawk. I hope it's not a vulture.

"Hey," I say. I think of all the stories I've heard about the lawlessness of the Ramseys. About the isolation of these hills.

Hale doesn't move. His arms are crossed. He's staring at me.

"Lot of work to set up a meeting," I begin. "I would have bought you breakfast."

"Say what you need to say."

"There's something I need to know. And there's something you need to know."

He works up a gob and spits at his feet. We're maybe 10 feet apart. "So say it," he says shortly.

In order for him to tell me what I need to know, I realize I'm going to have to give first. So I take a breath and plunge in. "It's about Brianna."

He snorts. "Tell me something I don't know."

"Why did you tell her you might go to the cops and let them know I was dealing drugs?"

This seems to catch him by surprise. "Never said no such thing. Ramseys don't turn on their friends."

It also squares with the Hale I know, the Hale who has been my friend through four long years of high school. I begin to relax.

"Well, she said you did. And she knew all about our little vitamin business, the runs to Des Moines. She said you were going to tell the police I was the one dealing."

Suddenly he looks interested. "Brianna said that? My Brianna? But she said you—"

"Tell me. What did she say about me, Hale? When you attacked my car, you said again and again, 'Deny it.' What was it you wanted me to deny?"

"That you were going to go to the cops and tell them I brought in the drugs."

I imitate Hale's hillbilly accent. "Never said no such thing. Larsons don't turn on their friends."

He studies me. Finally smiles to ease the tension.

"What else did she tell you?" I ask.

"What else?" He squints up at me. "Nothing."

I was afraid of that. It means, at the car back in Macon, he had wanted me to deny the drug thing. I had assumed he wanted me to deny I'd spent a night with Brianna.

So this is it, I realize. I've got to tell him. For the truth to come out about Sammy, *all* of the truth has to come out.

"Hale—"

"Let me show you something," he interrupts. "Remember I told you once about a mine shaft so deep that you can't ever hear a rock hit the bottom?"

I did remember. It was the place that legend had it the Ramseys had been dropping bodies of their enemies for generations.

"I want to show it to you," he says. "Step closer."

He points behind the bush that is somehow growing out of the rock. I see a hole. Maybe five feet wide.

Hale picks up a rock as big as a watermelon. Heaves it into the hole.

I listen. And listen. And listen.

All I hear is the slight breeze across the top of this knob of the mountain.

"See," he says. "Could be miles deep. Who knows what's at the bottom? Who knows how many secrets have disappeared in there?"

Again the horrible dragon of betrayal lurches around in the cave of my stomach. Hale doesn't know about Brianna and me.

"Hale, I—"

"I was so mad at you, I actually wondered if I'd be throwing you down there. I probably wouldn't have, but it hurt bad thinking about you turning on me. And I was afraid if I lost my temper hearing you out, that . . ." He points at the hole. "Probably not, though."

I shiver.

I'm going to have to tell him. But not yet. If I tell him now, he might actually kill me. Or at least shut down again and not tell me anything. And then I'll never know the answer to my burning question. Or what—if anything—I need to tell that detective.

"Brianna set us both up, Hale. She managed to turn us against each other. You know that, don't you?"

Hale nods again.

And I realize I'm right. That the theory that had been forming in my brain as I drove to Hazard County was solid. "Hale, Mitch was calling the shots. To divide us." I take a deep breath. "There's something I need to tell you, Hale. Listen and don't interrupt."

So I tell him about the night that Brianna showed up at the apartment and pretended that Hale had broken up with her. It took a long time to tell. I could barely look him in the eye.

"I'm sorry," I say. "Really sorry. Keeping it inside has been killing me."

He speaks softly. "So you'd rather let it out and have it kill me."

I think of the deep, bottomless hole that reaches to the bottom of the mountain. I can't defend myself, because there is no defense. But I know that Hale, too, is putting together the pieces. That he's realizing what I've come to realize.

"She gave you a white pill," he says. "With beer."

"A roofie."

He speaks slowly. "Just like she did to me. A few days after Sammy died. Called me to her place. Pretended everything was good again. And the next morning, I woke up in my Camaro."

I nod.

He's gotten it. Roofies. Guys sometimes use them on girls, knowing the girl won't remember anything that happened on the date. Brianna had used them on us the same way. Taken advantage of each of us. Not physically. But in a horrible way, just the same.

"That changes things, doesn't it?" Hale shuffles his right foot on the ground.

"Mitch is feeling pretty safe. He used Brianna to divide us. With us divided, he's safe against testimony."

"I don't feel divided no more," Hale says. "But he's still safe from testimony. There's a reason I'm in the hills. There's a reason I'm going to stay here until all of the trial is done. If I keep my mouth shut, I can't get in trouble."

"And Mitch skates free," I say.

"That will make two of us."

"Except Mitch can go on with his life. You'll always be hiding, wondering if someone's looking for you."

"Better hiding and free than in front of a judge. In case you don't remember, I don't exactly have a sparkling record when it comes to the law."

"But Sammy *died,*" I say. "Don't you care about that?"

"His decision," Hale counters, "to be at the party. His decision to take the drug. No one forced him to take it."

"His decision. But we're not innocent. I've decided I don't want it on my conscience," I say. "And Sammy was a friend. Remember when all the jocks were against us, and Sammy was the only one who wasn't? That he made high school at least bearable for us again? Doesn't that make you want to stand up for him? to tell what you know about what happened? Sammy deserves to have the truth come out. I can't change what happened, but I can change who I'm going to be from now on."

Hale looks surprised. It's probably the longest nonscience speech I've made in my life. And certainly the most passionate.

But he shakes his head. "So that means testifying to everything I did, like the drug deals. And I'd go back to that juvie center. No, I'd rather stay in hiding."

"No, Hale." I take a deep breath. "Just come back with me. We have to tell what we know about the drug deals. Sammy deserves that."

"It's your funeral," Hale claims.

"I just want to be able to walk tall when it's over," I say softly. "And right now I can't do that—not without telling what I know. I have to do what I know is right."

Hale's jaw tightens. "Well, I ain't going down that road. I'm not going to be somebody's roadkill. Too big a price to pay."

"I understand." I meet his direct gaze. "I just wish you'd change your mind."

Then I know it's time—time to ask the burning question I came all the way here to ask. "But, Hale, there's just one thing . . . one thing I need to know."

"So ask," Hale fires back.

"Did you give Sammy the Ecstasy, Hale?"

Hale doesn't answer. Just looks at me.

But his nonanswer is my answer.

I know our time together is over, and that I need to head back to Macon. But I've got a slight problem. I squirm. "You, um, got some money to lend me so I can put gas in my car and get back home?"

He laughs. Digs out his wallet.

I take a wad of cash. Promise him I'll send it back. He tells me to get Wanda's address and send it to her. He doesn't want anything to lead to him.

There seems to be nothing more to say.

I offer my hand, and he shakes it.

"See you," he says.

"Yeah," I say. "Take care."

Just like that, he leaves. Walks past the bottomless hole, down a path, and into the trees.

And I head back to Macon, Iowa.

Epilogue

Six weeks later, I'm sitting on a bench outside the courtroom, waiting for the trial to begin.

It's a big hall. Marble floors. High ceilings. Quiet
enough that the drumming of my fingers on the
bench seems to echo. I stop drumming my fingers.
After all, what do I have to be nervous about? I've
made my decision. I'm going to accept the consequences of my actions. I'm going to move forward.
It feels good.

I was the lost son. But I made the approach.

Turned back to the Father.

Held out my arms.

Gran was right. On that trip to Hazard, I had
finally felt the embrace of Someone who had been
waiting for me. Felt the embrace, just like the other
lost son. It was as simple as praying to Jesus. Confessing all I'd done, confessing how sorry I was.

242

And I felt the love. There's no other way to explain it.

In the quiet of that trip, I had pulled over onto the side of the highway. I had climbed out of the car and sunk onto my knees, right into the gravel. And there, at the side of the road, I had felt the love.

Since then things have changed. Yes, Sammy is still dead, and my father's still in prison. But things have changed between me and Gran. Between me and my father. I actually listened, without saying anything, when he phoned last week, instead of just hanging up right away. And, with Gran's urging, I've even begun to write my father a letter. I don't know what will happen between Dad and me, but at least it's a start.

In the last six weeks, since I've discovered the Father's love, I've also learned something else about love. Boy-girl love.

Kyra was an image to me. I loved who I thought she was. Not who she really was. Like loving a hologram. It might look real, but when you try to hold it, your arms go right through the image.

I wonder if it was that way for Sammy loving Miranda. And if maybe for Hale, it was the same thing with Brianna. If I ever see him again, I'll ask him about it.

I find myself smiling when I think about the boy-girl thing. After I sent a letter to Hale's cousin Wanda with money for Hale, she wrote back. And I wrote her back. We're starting to get to know each other. By telephone, e-mail, and letters. Much as I'd like to see her in person, this seems the right thing to do. I'm not distracted by projections of what I want her to be. I'm falling for her because of who she is.

A voice interrupts my thoughts. I'd been in my own world, so absorbed I hadn't heard the footsteps of the two men stopping in from of me.

"Look here." It's Mitch. In a suit and tie. Looking respectable. With an equally respectable man in a suit beside him, a man carrying a shiny leather briefcase. "It's the boy wonder, determined to make the world right."

The three of us are the only ones in the hallway.

I don't reply to Mitch.

"Won't work," Mitch says. "Your word against mine."

"Mitchell," the attorney growls. "Not here."

Mitch winks at me, then walks away.

At that moment I struggle not to hate the man who was the catalyst in Sammy's death.

But then I remember my own role. Because I chose to ignore what the "vitamin deals" really were, I had brought more drugs into the small town of Macon, Iowa. Drugs that had killed my friend Sammy. Even if I wasn't the one who had handed him the Ecstasy the night of the party, I was still guilty.

I know I will feel the weight of that guilt the rest of my life. And see it in Kyra James' eyes too.

No matter the consequences, I will do the right thing. I just hoped that Hale would too. But then we all have our degrees of guilt. And Hale would have to make the decision for himself. For Sammy.

Sneak Peek at Kyra's Story . . .

The phone rings as soon as we step into the house.
Mom picks it up. "Hello?"

I'm on the second step, heading upstairs, but I
can tell by Mom's phone voice it's a guy, probably
for me. She covers the receiver with her palm.
"Kyra, for you!"

"Who is it?" I ask.

"P.J. Something?"

She means D.J., and I don't feel like rehashing
Vin Diesel's career. I don't know if I want to go out
with D.J. again or not. "Tell him I'm not here!"
I call down.

Mom hollers, "Kyra?" She's against lies of the
bald-faced variety.

"Tell him I have a headache." It's the excuse
I gave Dad in the restaurant when he wanted me

to eat a roll. As soon as I say it, I realize it's true now. I really do have a headache.

I trot on upstairs. Mom will handle D.J. better than I could right now. She never wants to discourage any of them. If she only knew. . . .

I'm not sure what's wrong with me, why I don't feel like talking to D.J. or to anybody, why I don't want to think about school tomorrow, but then I *do* want to think about it.

Sammy's changed into sweats already and is headed back down the stairs, basketball in hand.

I block his path near the top of the stairs. "Sammy, do you still have your econ book from last semester?" I've put off economics as long as possible. Mr. Hatt will be the only teacher I haven't taken before. I want to make a good impression and get that over with. It would help if I could glance through the text before class.

"Yeah, right." Sammy bounces the ball on the stairs and then folds his long arms around it. "My beloved econ book is right beside my bed with my algebra book, framed." He fakes left and twirls past me on the right.

My muscles jerk in the pit of my stomach. I'm so tired of worrying about everything . . . and nothing. I don't want to think anymore, not about econ or school or D.J. or Vin Diesel. Not about anything.

I open the door to my room and wonder why it doesn't feel more like home, like *my* room. I got to choose new wallpaper last year, but I went with the one I could tell Mom was rooting for—

sky blue with slightly raised white puffs through it. It looks fine. I wouldn't have known what else to pick.

The desk is built in like a long counter with drawers on both sides. I never study there though. I sit on the floor or on my bed. The only poster, tack-mounted on my closet door, is the one Miranda gave me during her Beatles phase. John Lennon, looking so sad you could almost believe he knew what was coming.

I don't collect things like most of my friends. So the glass figurines on my wall shelf are things people have given me.

The CD tower by my bed is full, mostly with CDs guys have liked and given me or burned copies for me. When I dated Drew, I pretended to like the rap he ran through his car speakers, so he burned me about 20 rap CDs. Same with Dan, only he was into heavy metal.

I take the bottom CD without looking at it and stick it in my portable player. Then I plop onto my bed and lean back, facing the white, stucco ceiling.

I crank up the volume all the way before I put on the headphones. I like the surprise, the shock of sound when I slip on the headset. It's loud— head-shaking, teeth-jarring loud—like I've stepped inside a tunnel where I can't escape, but neither can the music.

Sneak Peek at Miranda's Story . . .

It's 10 minutes before fifth period when I get to school, and the halls are fairly vacant because kids are still at lunch. As I walk to my AP history class, it occurs to me that I could drop this class and still graduate. In fact, I could easily drop three classes and graduate. I only took these AP classes because Ms. Whitman said it would increase my chances of getting into a good college, possibly even on a scholarship. Funny how that used to be terribly important.

No one is in the classroom yet, and instead of finding a front seat, I go for the back row, far corner, next to the window. I open my history book and pretend to be reading, but my eyes don't focus on the page. I remember how I used to do this on a regular basis back in middle school—pretend to be invisible—and it usually worked. No one ever wanted to sit next to me or converse or even look at me back when I was a nobody. I want to be a nobody again. It shouldn't be that hard.

Kids are coming in now. I feel them looking at me, and I hear their whispers. I try not to imagine what they're saying, thinking. But I can't help myself. "There's the girl who killed Sammy James." Or "Can you believe she has the guts to show her face here, after what she did?" Or "Poor Kyra . . . she used to think Miranda was her friend."

I turn and look out the window, out across the back field where Taylor and Rebecca and I used to jog together for soccer practice, laughing and joking, back when I was human. Dylan is in this class. I hear him greeting Jamie, a boyfriend I once had—back in another lifetime. I can feel the two of them scrutinizing me as they find their seats. They are both too nice to say anything mean, but I can guess what they're thinking. They were both close to Sammy. Even though they go to church and claim to be good Christians, I'm certain they must both hate me. How could they not? *I* hate me.

About the Author

Sigmund Brouwer has written more than 50 novels for young adults and adults. In addition to *Tyrone's Story,* his young adult best-sellers include the ten heart-stopping titles in the Mars Diaries series (Tyndale). His acclaimed adult suspense-thrillers include the *Crown of Thorns, Out of the Shadows,* and *Lies of the Saints* (Tyndale).

It may appear that Sigmund's successes have unfolded as quickly as the plots in his fast-paced novels, but nothing could be further from the truth. In reality, his performance in high school English classes was so poor that he deferred his desire to write, choosing instead to earn a degree in commerce. But when a professor encouraged him, he earned a second degree in journalism—and his articles and short stories began appearing in Canadian and U.S. publications. Later, because of his love for sports, he served as editor of *National Racquetball* magazine.

Sigmund Brouwer and his wife, recording artist Cindy Morgan, and their daughter, Olivia, split living between Red Deer, Alberta, Canada, and Los Angeles.

www.thirstybooks.com
www.degreesofguilt.com